A collectic

Krampus and the Kolaches by JD Douwes

Werewolves Prefer Shortbread by Dakota Issacs

Luring the Lykan with Almond Macarons by Leslie Ann Brown

An Ounce of Spice

by

JD Douwes
Dakota Issacs
Leslie Ann Brown

An Ounce of Spice

COPYRIGHT © 2022 by The Wild Rose Press, Inc.

Cover Art by *The Wild Rose Press, Inc.*

The Wild Rose Press, Inc.
PO Box 708
Adams Basin, NY 14410-0708
Visit us at www.thewildrosepress.com

Publishing History
First Edition, 2022
Trade Paperback ISBN 978-1-5092-4509-3

Published in the United States of America

Krampus and the Kolaches

by

JD Douwes

Christmas Cookies Series

Dedication

To June, who is the best pal a person could want. To my critique partners who make everything better. To Molly for helping polish up the police scenes. To my kids for putting up with my crazy…well, everything. And, lastly, to Krampus: you'll always be my favorite.

Chapter 1

The sun is low in the gloomy sky, the light waning. Trees wrapped in holiday lights line the streets, large ornaments dangle overhead. Dina, Fred, and I are stopped in a line of cars in downtown Seattle, waiting for crowds of holiday shoppers and carolers on foot to pass us by. We've been waiting for five minutes easily. Oh well, it's Figgy Pudding; what are you going to do?

I'm singing a Krampus carol to pass the time. "God rest ye scary gentleman, let nothing you disdain," I sing, reading from the lyric folder on the torn seat next to me. Dina sings with me from the back seat, her voice soft and distinct.

I take a deep breath and launch into the next lyric, "Get in the way of your job today 'cause tomorrow's Christmas day." I gotta nail these lyrics.

Dina's kid Fred is looking out the window, his pale, freckled skin marred with a pimple right on the end of his nose.

I can almost see the entrance to the parking garage around the corner from our place in line. My nerves are getting more frayed by the minute, and it's not because pre-teen spirit and his mom are sitting behind me in the backseat with sullen gazes.

Harry hasn't answered my messages in two days, and the Figgy Pudding caroling competition is mere hours away. Without him dressed as Krampus, we'll just be ghosts. How do you explain ghosts singing naughty Christmas carols to a crowd of people looking for, well, *nice*? That and it's finally my chance to prove myself. It feels like high school all over again.

When I'm not singing, I'm telling myself, "It's fine, I'll be okay," on repeat. I need more time to memorize the carols we'll be singing with my ghost-hunting group, the NIGHT Crew. This is our first ever caroling competition. June's our strongest voice: a trained opera singer. Cindy can harmonize like a nightingale. But how can we pull this off without Harry?

My car is turned off; I'm a little low on gas, and it tends to overheat when I idle too long. Thankfully, it smells like heaven in here; a buttery sweet aroma drowns out the mildew odor and rank kid BO rampant in the air. Two dozen Apricot Kolaches cookies made from my oma's Christmas Cookie recipe are still warm in their plastic dollar store box beneath the caroling folder.

"Hey, Khalie? Gimmie a cookie," Fred says from the backseat, his voice cracking.

I check my hair and makeup in the rearview mirror, still singing, ignoring the pubescent kid in the back seat. I'd just put a red rinse over my dull dark-brown hair to try and give it a little more oomph. I look pretty hot tonight for a ghost.

"Give me a cookie!" Fred yells over our voices.

I angle the mirror and consider the cute red-headed kid in the back seat. "No, I'm sorry."

His hair is such a dark shade of red it's almost burnt orange. I'm kinda jealous. He's small for his age and almost cuddly-looking for a twelve year old. But, I had to borrow flour, sugar, cream cheese, butter, salt, and apricot preserves from my mom to make them. I already had the yeast, so that's good. No way am I going to waste them on *him*.

"Fred, those are for a charity bake sale. Remember?" Dina says in a voice better suited to a granny baby-talking her toy poodle. She shoves a strand of bleach blonde hair out of her eyes and continues, "Ms. Khalie told us when we got in. I'll grab you a cupcake on the way upstairs." She goes back to staring like a zombie out the window, listlessly singing. She is ankle-deep in fast food wrappers and empty coffee cups I probably should have tossed before they got in.

"No one's listening to me," Fred whines, undoing his seat belt.

His mom's hand shoots out, backhanding him into his seat. "You know better. Put your seatbelt on. That, right there, is a cop. You will *not* get me arrested again."

"Mom, I'm hungry. No one is going to miss a single cookie." He settles back but doesn't put his seat belt on.

"Nope. No cookie for you. Sorry, kiddo." I'm grateful we're almost there so I can get out of this car. Cute or not, kids are not my thing.

The police officer Dina mentioned stands one car in front of me, blowing his whistle to get passerby's attention.

"But I'm hungry," Fred whines, flinging his head back against the seat. Or at least that's what it sounds like. A short whistling sound that ends in an—

"Ouch!" I holler as an explosion of pain erupts in the back of my head—something hard ricochets off me and flies somewhere in the backseat with a clatter.

I press a hand to the painful spot and spin around; my other hand raised to swat at whatever hit me. "What the hell was that?" I search for the cause of my pain behind me. Did a bullet come through the window? But no, all our windows are intact. Dina's eyes are wide in surprise, and Fred is smiling back at me.

"What's wrong now?" Dina looks irritated.

"I don't know. Something hit me in the head."

Dina and I have been on a few ghost hunts together. She's constantly criticizing my EVP (electronic voice phenomena) sessions. Says my questions are stupid, and I make up shit that didn't happen.

"So, you automatically think it's us?"

Why did I agree to give them a ride again? I could have just *not* drawn a straw at our last meeting, saying I wasn't sure if my car would make it on the Seattle hills. It's not exactly a lie.

"It came from behind me, so that's where I looked. Sheesh, Dina, way to take care of a friend."

My phone pings with a text. I sit back down in my seat with the phone held low so the cop can't see it and type in my password. I'm sweating under all the layers of thrift store chic I'm wearing as part of my creepy costume.

It's a text from June. *—Have you heard from Harry? He's not answering my texts or private messages.—*

Just great. I shoot off a text and a private message to Harry. *—You'll get laid if you answer this message.—*

I have a chance to redeem myself here; finally, I get to sing in a choir. I'm hoping that the local news station will come by and record us singing. Can you imagine that? Me, on TV, singing! Take that, Mr. Paccar. Me, the kid you said would never be allowed to sing in a choir. If Harry shows up, that is.

Horns start blaring, and a voice from outside the car yells.

****

I look up to see the now angry policeman blowing his whistle so hard his face is beet-red. The man stops when he sees he has my attention. "Move along!" he yells, gesturing for us to drive forward.

Asshole. I take a deep breath. My first thought is to flip him off. I mean, can't he see I'm in pain? Instead, I give a curt nod, start the car, and complete my turn, taking the car into the parking garage. "Damn, that hurt. I wonder what it was."

Fred's breath tickles my ear. "It was this." He's leaning over the back of my seat. Out of the corner of my eye, I can see three or four stray stache hairs on his upper lip—and he's holding up his cell phone with an evil grin on his face.

"What… How?" I ask, shaking my head gingerly. "You know what? Don't answer." I palm his face and shove him back into his seat. "Everyone, just leave me alone." I focus as I drive through the tight turns. This garage is a brutal labyrinth, even on a good day.

He laughs quietly and flops back in his seat. "It just happened."

It's suddenly clear why everyone was relieved that I pulled the short straw to give Dina a ride.

Dina is still zoned out and staring out the rear passenger window, lips pouty. "Dina, are you hearing any of this?" She looks tired, and her light blonde hair is greasy and limp. Good thing she's going to cover it with a hat.

"Hm? What?" she says, seeming to wake up from a nap. "What's going on?"

"Your son just threw his freaking phone at my head."

"How dare you accuse my kid of doing something so awful. You don't know that's what happened."

"My God, Dina, he told me he did it." I navigate a turn.

She's wide awake now, her face a shade of red in my rearview mirror that can't be good. "Well, he has to be making it up. I can't believe you, of all people, would attack my son that way. He's had a hard life."

I slam on my brakes. Someone behind me screeches to a stop. They scream out their window and jam on their horn—this time, I give into my urge. I roll down the window, poke my head out, and hold out my hand, middle finger raised proudly. "Emergency, you cocksucker. You can wait," I scream. Surprisingly, they stop honking.

"My, my, aren't we over-reacting." Dina adjusts her seat belt.

"Me? Over-reacting? Give me your hand," I insist, turning in my seat and holding out my hand.

"No. What do you want my hand for?" She holds her hands to her chest.

"If you felt the damn egg growing on the back of my head, you'd believe me."

She rolls her eyes and pulls away from my flailing hand. "Oh, grow up."

"Your asshole son threw his phone at my head because I wouldn't give him a cookie. Go ahead, ask him."

Dina seems to be chewing on what to say next. My breathing is heavy as I wait for her to answer, my heart pounding.

A horn honks, almost as if it's unsure if it's the right thing to do. I flip them off again and start driving, returning to my search for June's car in the Puget Sound mall's parking garage.

A few seconds pass, and she says nothing. "Figures," I say, dropping it.

It's bad enough that my head hurts from getting smacked with a phone. I'm already frazzled about my first ever choir performance and having to park in downtown Seattle. These horribly designed parking garages, with their tight turns are nightmare inducing.

All of this plays through my head as I drive in circles through the garage, looking for June's red car. By the time I'm ready to turn around and go home, we finally see three familiar-looking people dressed in giant skirts gathered around a red car.

****

In the half-light of the garage, June, Cindy, and Marion stand next to the open hatch. I pull into the parking place next to them and get out of the car as fast as possible, the funky basement air hitting my cheeks.

"Here they are," Marion says. "Are you ready for Figgy Pudding?" She is. Her ghost makeup is on, and she's already dressed in a black eighteenth-century mourning skirt and blouse. A black hat is perched just so on her noble head.

"Hi, Khalie. You look great." June goes back to searching in the back of her car. Just like Marion, June looks out of place in this modern setting, dressed in a vintage black mourning gown.

I look down at my layers of faded, once-black blouses, my threadbare stretch pants, and thrashed discount store boots and grimace. "Um, thanks?" I open the trunk to retrieve the rest of our costumes and bags. It feels good to be out of the car finally.

Dina and Fred get out, slamming the car doors hard. Dina joins me at the rear of the car, lighting a cigarette with her hot pink lighter, relief on her face as she takes a long pull. She's dressed like me, so at least that makes me feel a little better.

Fred is on the side of the car, leaning against the driver's door. "Hold this." Dina shoves the lighter back in her bag and hands it to him. She comes back to me and goes about pulling on her hoopskirt and overskirt. The butt of her cigarette is wedged between pouty lips so she can use both hands, puffing it down in ecstasy.

I can see Fred through the windows, rooting around in Dina's purse. She either doesn't see it or doesn't care. The kid wears charcoal gray clothing. His skin is so pale against his dark orange hair he resembles the dead already. Maybe he'd be less of an ass as a ghost. I consider this as I pull on my hoopskirt. Nah, Fred will probably end up a poltergeist when he goes.

I check my phone. I've got three notifications. All from June, asking about Harry. She's busy going through a backpack, her round bottom facing us. "Hey June, sorry I didn't answer your texts. I was driving. I sent him some messages too, and he hasn't answered."

There's an irregular rhythm of cars driving overhead, helping my nerves uncoil as I type out another text message to Harry. Thoughts zoom through my mind as I safety pin a giant skirt over the hoopskirt. A strange clicking sound in the background punctuates each thought. *It's going to be okay.* Click. *Everything is going to be fine.* Click-click. *We're going to win.* Click. *I'm going to sing better than anyone.* Click-click.

"Anyone else hear that clicking sound?" I ask.

A few of them look around, saying, "Hear what?"

And "I can hear cars driving overhead." Still, Dina ignores me, having lit yet another cigarette off the butt of her last.

The sound continues. Dina says, "Fred, can you zip this up for me?" a cloud of smoke surrounding her. They're off to my left, near the others. The clicking stops for a minute.

I tug June's white Victorian wig into place, thankful that she's lending it to me, and look around. What is making that sound? Of course, it's silent again. Just a partially filled garage mostly devoid of life. Only us ghosts. The group is chatting as they wait for Dina and me to finish getting ready.

"Betcha Harry's not gonna show." Marion rests against her car. The clicking starts again. "Wait, is that what you're hearing?" She looks around. "I think I hear it."

"Mm-hm. Yeah, that's it," I say.

"Wouldn't surprise me if he doesn't." That's Dina. Bitch. She's next to June's car, done dressing. "Maybe I can hear the *click*? I'm not sure." Just like her son, she doesn't need to put makeup on to look dead. Fred is still on the passenger side of my car, doing God knows what.

I look around to see where the click's coming from but just see my crew strapping on elaborate hats.

"I know Harry's not perfect, but I still think you guys should give him another chance." I use the passenger window as a mirror to slather on a few more coats of white makeup.

"A man that grabs women's butts and blames it on getting drunk doesn't deserve a second chance." Marion shoves between Fred and June, her regal bearing making her look like the ghost of a posh aristocrat.

Fred leans into her touch and then jumps away, shaking her off as if she has cooties. "Stop it, you hag. Mom, she pushed me," he whines.

Dina rolls her eyes. "You're fine."

"You guys, stop bashing Harry. You know he's going to be here. He wouldn't leave us hanging like this." I carefully blot white powder around the eye makeup I'd spent hours applying earlier today.

Marion looks at me, dismissive, and pats her brown chignon. "Khalie, you know that man never keeps his word. Why do you always defend him?"

"She likes bad boys." Cindy shakes perfect dark-brown ringlets off her face. She looks at June, who has just finished smudging black eyeliner around her eyes to finish her ghostly look. "Do we have a plan B?"

My face gets hot. "He's super sweet. He cleaned my mom's gutters for her right before the freeze hit." I shoot off another text to Harry and go back to dabbing on makeup. It's not easy getting just the right shade of white.

"A right saint." June shakes her white wig-covered head and holds her phone up in different directions as if trying to catch a rogue beam of internet. She's got a crap phone provider.

"Cleaning leaves out of gutters does not make up for all the times he's stood us up," Dina says.

"Isn't Cindy the tallest? She should be the one to wear the Krampus costume," Marion says.

Cindy stands at least half a foot above the rest of us. One of her perfect eyebrows is arched in disgust. "Oh no, you don't," she says. "Can you imagine having a hot flash in that costume?" She waves to June's car, where good ole Krampus's costume rests.

Out of the corner of my eye, I can see that Fred is inching closer and closer to me. What the hell? He's flicking his hand like he's trying to snap. What an odd way to keep yourself busy.

"Need to find a restroom," Marion says. "Be back pronto." Her back is artificially straight as she stalks off like she's got a stick up her butt.

That strange clicking is driving me crazy. I'm about ready to do a full-on search for it when the aroma of something burning wafts up. I'm sweating again, which is weird, being underground in a cement jungle and all. And then I look down and see smoke.

"Where is that smoke coming from?" June is looking down past my bargain boots. "Is it coming from your car?"

I crouch down and check, my skirt poufing out behind me—That's when everyone starts talking loudly at once.

Chapter 2

First, it's just June. "Khalie, your skirt!" Her shrill voice is coming from my left. And then everyone chimes in, shouting things I can't understand. All I can see is smoke and the cement floor and the undercarriage of my car—A body flies at me, slamming me into my bumper, taking me down to the ground with them. The side of my face slams into the concrete—a searing pain lighting up my sight.

I crane around to see Cindy lying on top of me, her dark ringlets askew. Up close, her skin is porcelain-perfect. "Got it," she calls out, breathing heavy.

The weight of the tackle takes my breath away, so when she crawls off, I'm left wheezing. "What happened?" I ask, rolling over, trying to see what I look like in the chrome of my bumper. The distorted image tells me nothing.

"Your skirt was on fire." There's something brown and furry in her hands.

"What did you put the fire out with?" June asks, her eyes wide open.

Cindy holds up the Krampus costume, a melted patch of fur next to the tail. "Harry's costume. It was the first thing I found."

June's lips part in a silent scream. After a beat, she breathes in through her nose. "I just spent over a hundred dollars on updating that costume. It's ruined." Her voice is quiet, her full cheeks blazing red through pale face makeup.

Cindy brushes herself off and takes a look at the costume. "It's not that bad." She scrubs her fingers over the singed fake fur. "He's supposed to be from hell, anyway."

June sniffs. "We'll make it work. How did Khalie's skirt catch on fire?" She scans the ground, looking for evidence.

"I don't know." I take a closer look at the Krampus costume. It looks like Sasquatch backed into a campfire, melting his butt fur. "The Krampus costume's fine. No one will notice." I look around where I'm puddled on the ground searching for something that could have ignited my costume.

"So strange." June straightens up.

"I don't see anything that could have caused it." I stand carefully, looking at myself in the window again. The side of my face is scraped bloody. My eyeliner is smeared, and there's a glob of garage dirt on my cheek. Is that Dina's cigarette butt stuck in my hair? Well shit.

June heaves a heavy sigh, holding her phone high over her head again, seeming to pray to the internet gods. "Did Harry get back to you yet?"

"Maybe." I check my phone. It pinged a few times while they were dissing Harry. My headache from the knot on the back of my head has graduated to a throbbing, almost migraine.

With a cool hand to my forehead, I squint at my screen. It's cracked from the impact of getting body-slammed to the cement floor, but I can still see through the webbed glass that I have seven notifications. Each one has a red warning sign next to it. "My texts and social

13

media messages didn't go through. No internet connection down here." My phone service isn't great, either.

"Darn it," June whispers, shoving things back into a bag with a delicate touch. Louder, she says, "We better finish up and get up there."

"Let me try to get cleaned up." I look over my shoulder to see the damage from the fire. "How bad does my skirt look?" I ask, angling it toward the group.

"Don't clean up too much. You can say you're a ghost from the Great Seattle Fire of 1889." Cindy drags her signature blood-red lipstick over her mouth.

"Gee, that makes me feel so much better." I dive back onto my makeup bag for some emergency makeup repair.

About five minutes in, footsteps pound on the pavement, coming from the elevator bay. There's a strange back-note of a *clip-clop* going on at the same time. I look up, expecting to see someone running with a pony or a kid playing with a toy or something. But no. That's not what's coming toward us.

Marion holds her skirts high as she runs down the parking aisle toward us. "Harry isn't responding," she says between labored breaths, "and I checked us in with the coordinator. We're in space J." She's panting and holding out a slip of paper with a map on it.

June reaches out for it with an elegant hand, and the rest of us lean in to see where they've placed us. "Are we in the middle of the intersection?"

"They have the streets barricaded off—" Marion breaks off, staring down at my skirt. "What the hell happened to you?" She may look like a lady, but she fits in perfectly with the rest of us when she talks.

Everyone speaks at once: "It caught on fire!" "You wouldn't believe it!" "So much smoke."

The irregular *clip-clop* stopped when Marion got here, but it starts again. Somewhere in between a gallop and a trotting sound. I crane around, leaving the rest behind to see where it's coming from.

A man ambles toward us dressed in a giant brown furry costume with horns, chains wrapped around his body. My spirits rise, happiness bubbling to the surface.

"Harry!" I squeal and run toward him.

****

When I make it to Harry's side, I throw my arms around his barrel chest, my hands landing on the wicker basket he's carrying on his back. A waxy musk odor hits me square in the face. I squint, the scent so strong I have to pull my head away. But he feels so solid and comfortable in my arms. I mean, the smell *is* a little…I don't know. Muskier than usual?

"New cologne?" I whisper and give him one more squeeze before letting go. Even with the new cologne, I like what this costume does for him. "I knew you'd make it," I say louder this time for everyone to hear.

He narrows his eyes, the mask so real I'm stunned. Wow, June really did put some money into this thing. A low growl rises from what sounds like the ground, so I back up fast. "How are you doing that?"

"Where is the boy child?" Harry growls, evading my question. When he says 'where,' the word has a 'v' at the beginning instead of 'w.' I mean, I know he was practicing getting into character, but since when does Krampus have a Russian accent?

"Fred?" I look back to where the rest of my group stands. He must be hiding because I can't see him. "He's here somewhere."

Harry's mask moves like he's wearing makeup and prosthetics from the movies instead of a clumsy rubber thing.

Wait a minute. "You had Steve do your makeup! You look amazing!" I'm proud of myself for figuring it out. Steve did a fantastic job. He must have had another costume for Harry to wear, too, because the butt-singed pants are still in the back of June's car.

Steve is part of our ghost hunting group, and I'm sure he's gonna end up in Hollywood someday with his makeup skills. I pull on Harry's arm and start making my way back to our group. Man, this costume gives him great biceps.

It looks like Cindy is tracking our progress back to the cars, a judgy look on her face. We're only two cars away when I say, "Anyone see Fred?"

Dina is with June at the back of June's car, and Cindy and Marion stand by mine. Footsteps pound the cement floor off in the distance, followed by the ping of the elevator. Weird, I didn't see anyone else here.

All five of us look at each other, then around. June shakes her head slowly at first and then with conviction as she looks around each car. "Dina? Where's little Freddy?" Her words are laced with doubt.

"He's over here." Dina breaks away from the group and goes over to where I'd last seen him making that flicking motion next to my car. Even from here, I can see there's no Fred.

"That little monster, where'd he go?" Dina pouts in concentration as she texts madly. A second passes, everyone holding their breath, and then her phone gives a tiny ping. She looks at the incoming message and tilts back her head, letting out a wail of torment. No internet. "Fred, if you don't get back here right away, you're dead!" she screams.

It doesn't take a second wail for everyone to realize what's going down. We shout out quadrants of the parking garage for each person to scout, with Harry and me left next to the cars, waiting in case Fred comes back.

"Time is if the essence. We must find the child." Harry's ears are fascinating, almost moving like a cat's.

"Wait, how do you do that?" I ask, reaching up to touch them, but he's so tall they're out of my reach. "Is there some kind of internal control?"

"What absurdity are you talking about?" he asks, taking a step away, a stern look on his face.

"How do you move your ears like that?"

He shakes his head, impatient. "It is of the most importance to finish my mission. I have a long list to get through."

"Dude, I'm very familiar with the Krampus myth lore. I know he's Santa's best bud and that he handles the naughty list. I don't need the educational chit-chat."

"The child—" he starts to say, but I cut him off.

"We *are* looking for the child, right now, in fact. Chill."

Harry squints at me while what looks like a million responses run through his mind. He leans on my car; it squeaks and starts to roll, making my heart skip a beat, but then stops when the breaks stick.

We can hear variations of the kid's name getting called out from every direction. After a handful of minutes, everyone comes jogging back, shaking their heads.

"Couldn't find him," Marion says.

"Me either." June bends over, hands to knees, wheezing.

I can tell by Dina's glassy eyes and knit brow that this isn't good. Is that panic turning her face red?

"We need to find him. Everyone split up." Dina claps her hands to get our attention.

****

We're standing in a semi-circle around Dina, the cars behind us.

"June and Khalie, go to the cupcake store and then check out the first and second floors."

"I need to get my cookies to the bake sale," I say, but she keeps going.

"Cindy and Marion, you go check the third and fourth floors, including the movie theater."

Cindy frowns. "Got it."

"Shouldn't we go upstairs and call the cops?" Marion asks.

Dina's eyes widen. "No. We can't call the cops." She turns to Harry. "You're with me. We'll check out the streets surrounding the mall and then wait at our space, letter J. I swear he was here when we were talking about what space we're at, so maybe he'll just meet us there." She's talking so fast that you'd think she's had too much caffeine. "I need the internet, and that's the best place to get it."

"Um, Dina? Can I be paired with Harry?" I ask.

June smiles and flutters long lashes at me. "What, I'm not good enough for you?"

"You know I love you, June, but I need to…talk to Harry for a bit."

Dina taps her foot in impatience. "Fine. June, you're with me." Dina turns to Harry, who is looking away, his ear tilted to the side. "Harry?" I had no idea costumes can move so realistically. She pokes him, and he finally looks back at her. "You're with Khalie."

My heart leaps in joy. I'm proud to be at Harry's side, especially with how good he looks in this costume. He's so tall, with his shoulders drawn back, head held high. I think I'm warming to his new cologne, too.

"Let's go, let's go, let's go." Dina claps her hands, greasy hair bouncing.

There is a chorus of agreements as the rest of us shove on our hats and grab our things, arming the car alarms.

With my backpack and bag in hand, I head off with Harry at my side. His costume is so soft. I'm staring lasers into Cindy's back as she walks in front of us, swinging her hips. June and Dina trail behind.

About halfway to the elevators, my foot lands on uneven ground, and I stumble. Harry's hand—or should I say paw?—shoots out with lighting speed and grabs my outstretched arms. He effortlessly helps me to steady myself. Wow, he's even gotten manners since I've seen him last time.

"Thank you," I say. Harry nods gallantly, deep in character. His acting lessons are paying off.

I readjust my backpack over my shoulder and inspect the ground below me. There's a hot pink lighter on the cement floor. I kick it aside, my brain spinning. Isn't that the same lighter Dina used to light her cigarette?

Fred's ghostly white face flicks across my mind, that smirk of his confirming who the lighter belongs to. "Fred!" My brain is going to explode. "That little shit!" I shriek, and everyone looks at me.

19

"What *are* you going on about?" Marion calls out from a few steps ahead of us.

I puff my chest out. "Dina's little monster is the one who lit my skirt on fire!"

The word 'fire' falls flat against the soundproofing in the garage, but a lone person walking by looks at me, alarmed, then hurries off. Lesson learned: this is *not* the thing you want to say out loud in a place with good acoustics.

"What did you say?" Dina whirls around, squinting, her arms crossed across her faded black ruffled blouse. Harry and I are smack in the middle of my group, with Dina and June behind us. Everyone except for Dina is nodding in recognition.

Marion thrusts her shoulders back. "Your kid is out of control, Dina. He lit Khalie's skirt on fire. You need to handle him."

A shrill sound escapes Dina's full lips. She stomps her foot and stalks off.

"Fancy of you to finally make it," June says to Harry. She giggles, her delicate hand flying over her mouth. "I'm sorry, did I say that out loud? I *meant* to say, 'So glad you could make it!'" She goes around us on her way to follow Dina.

"We should get moving." Cindy sashays after June.

They are waiting at the elevator when we get there. June glances up at us through the black veil she's pulled over her face. "You guys, the judges will be stopping by—" She looks at the piece of paper in her hand. "—at five twenty. It's four thirty-one. We need to find Fred fast."

Dina stares at the ground, ignoring us. What a drama queen.

I roll my eyes and sigh, tugging on Harry, who looks like he's ready to walk away. "You coming? We need to find the kid before we go to our spot." I point up.

Harry gives off a breath-grunt. "I do not have time to waste. I must find the child before it's too late." The word 'waste' comes out like 'vayst,' somewhere between a Russian and German accent. At least he's trying to make his costume come off more authentic. Krampus is from German folklore, right along with Hansel and Gretel, though he's featured in other cultures as well.

"Whoa, take a chill pill there," I say. "We're trying to locate him."

Harry grunts again, but he bends his head to get on the elevator with us when an empty one finally stops on our floor.

****

We barely fit in the elevator with our hoopskirts and giant hats, never mind the bags we are toting along with us. The ceiling is so low that Harry has to crouch. Almost everyone starts sniffing and giving Harry the side-eye, his cologne so strong.

"Why does it smell like cat litter in here?" Marion asks, her face scrunched up in confusion.

"I don't smell anything weird." I'd be offended, I mean, he *is* my boyfriend, but he barely changes the cat litter at his house. It's not surprising that he'd smell like a litter box.

Seeing Harry stand next to Cindy is eye-opening. He's over a foot taller than her. I remember lying in bed curled up at his side as he talked about making special stilts to fit inside the Krampus costume pants. I just didn't know he had the skill to make them. He's more of

21

a dreamer than a doer, usually.

Everyone is silent and tense for most of the ride. I'm singing inside of my head, trying to remember the lyrics to our Krampus carols and failing madly. Probably because my head hurts from this whole fiasco. Harry looks around, his eyes wild, ears down as if planning his escape. Those ears are badass.

When the door slides open, we're greeted by people trying to board our car. Their mouths drop open when Harry lurches out, and all but one scatter. Five ghosts and a man in an extremely convincing Krampus costume probably make a disturbing sight. June, Dina, and I file out of the elevator, excuse me, pardoning me, our way. Marion and Cindy stay behind on their way to the third floor, both glaring after us.

"Meet us at space J by five twenty," June calls over her shoulder, rushing after Dina, who is almost running.

I break free from the crowd entering the elevator to find Harry, looking around the first floor. I put my hands on his lower back and gently shove, but he doesn't even look at me. "Come on. We need to get searching."

He swivels his head slowly, seeming to sniff the air. "Where has the child gone?" he asks, again with more Vs replacing his Ws. Actors. What are you going to do with them?

"Seriously? We're trying to figure that out. Follow me." I tug on his arm. Does he have to be in character all the time? I mean, I know that folklore says that Krampus is after kids on the naughty list, but this is getting annoying.

We find our way to the cupcake booth, guided by the scent of chocolate icing and something I can't define. Thankfully we're the only customers. I can't take any of the comments I know are coming our way about our costumes.

There's one employee behind the counter, her eyes wide. Her eyes narrow as she sniffs the air, a confused look on her face. I can't blame her. I mean, Harry looks like something in-between a goat, a man, and a dog—and he smells like that too. He's seriously freaky looking, pressed against the booth, leaning over the counter. I'd be scared too.

"What delicacies do we have here?" he asks, a soft repetitive thrumming sound beginning. "Sweets are my weakness." He's so tall with the added benefit of the stilts that when he leans over the glassed-in area, he's able to get his nose right up close and personal with the cupcakes. "Smells delectable." He sniffs each cupcake in turn. His entire costume is shaking from that sound.

The employee backs up, trembling, her face gone white. "Sir, you can't do that. Please step back."

I'm going to die of embarrassment. I grab Harry's elbows from behind and pull him backward. "I'm sorry, we're here for the Figgy Pudding caroling competition. He's dressed as Krampus—are you familiar with that folktale?" I ask, hoping to assuage her fears. "He's just getting a little bit too much into character."

The employee shakes her head, the look on her face unaltered.

"Harry, come on now. Stop playing around. You're scaring the poor girl." Why is he hamming it up so much?

He takes a small step back, his head and ears lowered, seeming to heed my warning. "What is the name of these confections?" he asks, his tongue lolling, eyes sliding up and down the selection of cupcakes.

This makeup is fantastic. What is making his costume shake like that?

"Cupcakes." The word escapes the woman's mouth like a hiccup. She's pressed against the back counter, trying to stay as far away from us as possible.

"I must have one." He's almost panting. That thrumming kinda sounds like he's purring, only extra loud. It's coming from the middle of his back.

Wait a minute.

I put my head against his back, the sound intensifying. "It's a motor!" Makes sense. I mean, something needs to control the movement of the ears. He's too preoccupied to answer. A gurgling sound joins the thrum.

Maybe it's his stomach growling. "Are you hungry?"

He nods, his eyes glossed over, and he inches closer and closer to the shop gal again. The vibration is getting louder and louder beneath my ear. It has to be a motor; the sound is too big.

I step to the side. His tongue is back in his mouth, but he's drooling, the pink tip of his tongue sticking out between yellowed, gnarly-looking teeth. Steve must have given him fake teeth. Harry's natural teeth look like tiny ceramic tiles.

I pull him back a bit. "Don't drool on them." His mouth must be watering because of the teeth. I can relate; I drool when I wear my retainer.

I glance at the employee and force a laugh. "You wouldn't happen to have seen a red-headed kid about this high." I hold my hand to my nose.

The employee nods rapidly, her look of shock at Harry's boldness changing to anger. "Yes! He snuck behind the counter and stole a cupcake not too long ago."

Harry's eyebrow is arched when he looks at me, his eyes puppy-dog wide. "May I have a cupcake?"

"Sure, you can buy one," I say. Why does he expect me to pay for everything?

He pulls his wicker bag from his back to his side, the one the birch branches are nestled in. After plunging his hand in for a minute or two, he comes out bare-handed. "My apologies, my lady. I did not come prepared." A thin, keening sound follows. It takes me a second to realize he is whining like a dog.

I roll my eyes and shove my hand in the cookie bag, thrusting a crumpled ten-dollar bill on the counter. "You owe me." I count backward from the money I'd brought with me to pay for dinner. That's going to take off a pretty chunk.

"Which one do you want." I point at the deserts.

"Only one?" he asks. This man is going to kill me.

"He'll take that one." I point at one with a swirl of cream cheese frosting and sprinkles on top. I look at him. "I always get Carrot Walnut."

"Oh, come on, try something new!" The employee seems to have gotten over the shock of her strange customers. "How about the Triple Chocolate? At least it won't show up on his costume."

Harry's eyes light up, so I nod. "Okay, we'll take the Triple Chocolate."

We watch, me patiently and Harry salivating as the lady packages up the cupcake. That purring-motor sound gets loud again.

"Did you see which direction the redhead went?" I hold my hand out for the change.

The girl tugs on her apron. "Um, I think he went that

way." She points to the bookstore.

"Okay, thanks. My change?" I ask, resting my hand on the counter.

"I'm sorry, ma'am, but I need to get paid for the cupcake your little friend stole. They'll take it out of my paycheck if I don't."

Dina is so going to hear about this.

"Okay, fine. Whatever." I try to tug Harry away, but again, he's staying put. He stuffs his face into the box she hands us and chomps down on the whole dessert, paper and all.

"What are you doing?" I ask, grabbing at the cupcake paper that's dangling out of his mouth.

He lets me take the paper, then swallows with a contented sigh. "That was delightful. May I have more?" he asks, taking a step to the counter.

"No. We need to go," I say. "Did you even chew it?"

The employee scoots back to her previous post, staring at us wild-eyed.

"Maybe these?" he asks, pulling the box of apricot kolaches from beneath my arm with care, his gloved hands adorned with long claw-like fingernails, not even making him clumsy. How can he be so graceful—and sneaky, in such an awkward-looking costume?

"Stop it." I yank away the box and stuff it back in my bag. "The longer we mess around, the harder Fred is going to be to find."

Harry seems to understand where I'm going with this. He stands up tall and begins sniffing the air again, his ears moving in every direction. This costume is surreal. "What direction did the child go?" he asks.

"She said he went this way." I point to the bookstore across the lobby.

His bushy eyebrows join, and his eyes narrow as he looks around. The motor's purr has stopped.

"C'mon," I say, heading toward the bookstore.

Chapter 3

Silent Night plays over the mall's sound system, and I sing along softly, stopping at every store to do a quick look-through for the kid. I'm singing the lyrics that we'll be performing tonight: 'Silent night, deadly night,' in place of the traditional words. Harry waits outside of each store, keeping an eye out for the kid. Why is this my responsibility? I mean, Dina could have left the little shit at home.

Harry isn't waiting for me when I leave the last store before the bookstore. I can see him a hundred yards away or so, his wicker basket bouncing off his back and chains rattling as he looks around. I need to do something about my headache, so I sit on a bench and search through my bag and backpack for some headache medicine. There has to be at least one in here somewhere. In the back of my mind, I can hear Dina's wail at Fred's disappearance. My stomach tightens into a knot. Why the hell am I looking for her kid when I need to be practicing Krampus carols?

Finally, I find a grimy, almost destroyed packet of headache medicine and pop a few in my mouth, dry swallowing them. I'm so thirsty but getting out of this costume to pee is going to be a bitch, so I'm not risking it.

I've just shoved the empty medicine packet in the bag when people start to squeal. A now-familiar *clip-*

clop signals Harry's return, along with a high-pitched scream. He's trotting toward me, chains clinking. His eyes are wild, and his costume's goat-like horns are more pronounced because of his flattened ears. An old lady is splayed on the ground behind him, hand to chest, and children are running away crying. I shake my head. He doesn't look that scary, sheesh.

"What did you do now?" I ask. He's such an attention whore.

"The child isn't here either." Harry stops at my side. The hard 'th' makes it come out 'e-der.'

"No kidding." I stand up. "Let's check out the bookstore before we get kicked out." He doesn't hesitate, trotting after me.

Inside the store, I ask, "You're taller than I am. Can you see a red-headed kid?"

Harry raises to his full height and looks over bookcases with narrowed eyes. We can hear a gasp or two—probably people seeing him for the first time. His ears are cocked in different directions while he sniffs the air and looks around. I'm in awe of how fantastic he looks in this costume. Damn. Maybe I have a thing for tall men. Or maybe Cindy's right. Maybe it's just the fact that Krampus is one of the baddest boys there is, the costume amping up Harry's sex appeal.

"Anything?" I ask.

"No red-haired child."

Of course. "Okay, let's see." We've made it to a sign boasting the store map. "Let's try the children's area." I point to the stairs going up. "We can hit the second floor of the mall after that."

He takes off at a break-neck speed up the steps, his hooves so loud I swear everyone in the store turns around and looks at us. I try to follow him as fast as I can muster, kicking myself for giving this man sugar. Clearly, it's like speed to him.

Once I finally make it up to the kid's area panting and even more sweaty, I almost run into him. He's stopped at the top, like a great white shark searching for its prey. A thirty-something dad sits in an armchair with a young kid on his lap. Harry is fixated on them, his eyes softer than I've ever seen them.

The child is sleepy, rubbing his eyes, and the dad is so tender with him that my heart twinges.

Harry looks down at me, resting his long taloned hand on my shoulder. "What's wrong?" There's that accent again, making it come out like 'vuts vrong.' Ups his sex appeal times ten. I wonder if I can talk him into using it when we're in the bedroom? Or backseat of the car. I'm not picky.

I shake my head to rid myself of the warring emotions of attraction and sadness. Jutting my chin at the father-son duo, I say, "My dad sucked. He never played with me, let alone read me a book."

Harry's eyes are dreamy like he's lost in a memory. "That is a sad tale. My father was a good man. He worked a lot, but we frequently played when he was home. Unloved, I never felt." How does he hold on to the accent for so long? I kinda love it, but really.

"Huh." I try to imagine the man I'd met at Thanksgiving playing with anyone, let alone kids. Harry's dad scratched his crotch and guzzled beer while screaming at a football game on TV the whole time we were there. Harry acted like it was expected, sidestepping the Barcalounger where his dad sat in the family room to hug his mom and Nanna. Maybe Harry was hiding his softer side from me.

Someone shoves past us as they come upstairs, breaking our trance.

"Let's keep moving," I say. Harry nods and resumes his search, looking over the bookshelves. We wander through the aisles, encountering a few kids who stare up at him, eyes wide, backing away in what looks like fear. A few adults scream and grab their kids and start running from us as we pass.

"So, do you see him?" I ask.

"No red-headed child," he says.

"Okay then, let's try something else." We continue to walk the perimeter of the store. I'm trying all the places I'd have gone to as a kid. The next one up is the bathrooms. Because where better to shove stolen merchandise beneath your clothes? Not that I'd know or anything.

I have Harry duck in to check the men's room, and I do a quick search of the women's room. Nothing.

We don't have any luck in the candy and toy areas strewn throughout the store. Fifteen minutes of tearing around looking for the little shit, and nothing.

Harry glances at me, eyebrows joined as he runs a long talon over the second-floor map, searching for the exit to the mall.

"Sir? Miss? We've had some complaints about you." A man wearing a green polo stands before us; a black lanyard with his credentials hangs from his neck. "It's against store policy to wear masks that cover your whole face while in the store. We'll need you to leave."

"Excuse me, sir, but surely we're allowed to look for a lost little boy." Can I crawl under the carpet now?

The expression on the young man's face changes.

"I'm sorry, but you're scaring our customers. You have to leave. I can contact mall security for you and have them meet you at the exit. Give me a description of the kid and your cell number, and I'll pass it on to them in case you have trouble finding each other."

The employee keeps stealing glances at Harry, his upper lip curled, eyes narrowed.

I grab the notepad he pulls out of his breast pocket and scribble the information he requested. "Is it against policy to show us where the exit to the mall is?" I grab Harry's hand. It feels so good in mine. So real, even though it's part of the costume he wears.

We're escorted to the door to the mall, finding ourselves on yet another search for the kid.

What a night.

Forget about mall security. Maybe it's time to call the cops.

****

The second floor of the mall is wide open in the center, with a walkway around its periphery. Beyond the railing, we can look down on the first floor below us and up to the two levels above. It kinda reminds me of an apartment complex or a motel, only there's a roof over our heads. Everything is in shades of glistening whites and grey, from the floor to the walls. A huge Christmas tree soars up from the food area below us, the star at eye level from up here. Over-sized stuffed animal reindeer in mid-flight hang from the ceiling, guiding an equally stuffed Santa and his sleigh.

Harry stares at it in wonder. "Santa," he calls out, waving.

I've never seen him use his acting skills in public before; I'm muted by embarrassment, looking between him and Santa.

"Hey, Santa, it is I, Krampus." He cups his hands around his mouth. His voice carries through the open mall, and again we're the center of everyone's curiosity. He must have been watching that Arny Swartzen-whatever guy's Christmas movie or something.

I hit him. "Stop it. Everyone's looking at us." Thankfully this level of the mall has fewer people, so he's a little less conspicuous. If you can call a seven-and-a-half-foot man wearing a sasquatch-goat hybrid costume inconspicuous.

He looks around and then shakes his head. "That is to be expected. What is not is why Santa ignores me. I haven't seen him in a fortnight, what with his Yule preparations. I had not thought he'd be upset that I did not interrupt him."

Wait a minute here. "Are you high?" I lean in to take another sniff of his musky scent. Nope, I don't smell weed.

"What is this high you speak of?" he asks, distracted.

Whatever. "Listen, we've just been kicked out of a bookstore for looking too creepy. We're minutes away from having to be at our post, and instead of warming up my voice, I'm searching high and low for this stupid little shit." My voice is getting higher and higher as I talk. "Can you just cut the crap?"

"Why do you worry about your voice?" he purrs, scratching the luscious hair on his mask with his costume nails. "When you speak, your words are melodious." He grabs my wrist and guides me along.

I stumble to keep up, my heart softening. "Thank you. But the singing competition is a big deal to me."

He nods, sniffing in each direction. "Why?"

"You know those aptitude tests they make you take when you're a freshman in high school?"

Harry shakes his head. "No. I received tutoring at my opa's."

"Wait, how did I not know that about you?"

He gives me a squished-face shrug. "Go on."

"Well, it's this test that is supposed to guide you to a career choice. Only mine came up with a less than average aptitude for every single thing it tested for."

"Master of none." He nods in understanding.

"But I love to sing. That wasn't on the test. So, mom got me a singing coach for Christmas to cheer me up."

He stops in front of a store. "Just a moment. Go inside and check for the child. I shall wait," he says, ever on task.

I do what he says but don't see Fred anywhere. "Nope," I say when I come back. He nods.

"A singing tutor?"

"Yes, and for the next two years, we scraped by, saving every penny for my dream of becoming a famous singer."

We've stopped at another store. I hold my finger up to signal I'd continue in a minute and go in. Harry stays outside, but we get the same result. No kid.

"Have you yet achieved this fame?" he asks.

I start laughing. "Oh my God, no. I work at the customer service desk at Dormart. You know that." I swat him.

"What became of your dream?"

We stop in front of another store. Again, I hold up my finger and repeat the process, with the same result: no kid.

We continue walking. "I auditioned for the choir at school and didn't get in. The choir leader said no one would ever let me sing in public with my nasal voice. And that was it." I shrug. "So, I gave up."

"I will send him to hell for you." Harry gently puts his large hand on the small of my back. He steers me inside yet another store.

I laugh and complete my task. When I come back out, we continue our search. "Thanks. But that's what tonight is about. My second chance. But here we are, wasting time looking for this stupid kid, and I'm not ready for the competition."

"We must make haste." He guides me along the walkway.

We spend the next few minutes practically running through the second floor of the mall. When we're finally done, we trot down the stairs to the first floor.

"Look, I need to get to the competition. I know you want to find the kid. Please come with me. It won't make sense if you're not there. Our dark music is mostly about Krampus and stuff like that, remember?"

He shakes his head, looking confused.

Had he never read the lyrics? I mean, his costume should have given him a clue. "Okay. Whatever. But can we take a break from our search and get the competition out of the way?"

What I want him to say is, "Let's just go. He'll show up." Because that's legit what I'm thinking. The thing is, we're due at space J in fifteen minutes, and I need to get my kolaches cookies to the bake sale before everything begins.

"Regrettably, I must find the child. The list cannot wait."

"Enough of the method acting, bud." My anger flares back up. Why doesn't he ever put me first? "I'm done looking for him." I'm trying to look him in the eye, but he's so tall.

"I cannot go, but you must not miss your competition. I'll carry on. We shall meet again," Harry says.

Kinda a fancy way to say, 'meet you at our space,' but I'll take it. My gaze falls on a blob of icing on his neck. How can he be so clean he has to shower before and after sex but not even notice that he's got food on his neck? Well, costume, but still.

"You've got a little icing in your fur," I say. There are cupcake crumbs all over the fur on his neck and chest too. "Here, let me wipe this off for you."

He crouches just enough that I can reach easier, turning his gaze to me. His eye color morphs from brown to hazel as he puts his hand on mine. "Thank you, my lady."

I grab a napkin out of my bag to wipe him off. "No problem." He's giving me butterflies standing this close, his breath so sweet. It's hard to be mad at him.

"You are different than the other women in this time," he says in a soft voice.

I brush his neck with the back of my fingers, and he leans into my touch, his eyes closed. I'm so caught up in the moment that I'm almost cooing when the motor-purr starts again. "That's the problem." I suppress the urge to kiss the remaining crumbs away.

"You are one of a kind." He takes my hand and kisses the palm.

His lips on my hand send chills down my spine. My phone pings over and over again. I glance at it, seeing a

flood of group messages, the most recent, variations of
—*We're at our spot, no Fred.*—

"Well, maybe I have time for one more search."

Chapter 4

Harry pushes the door open for us, allowing me to go first. Such a gentleman. This isn't like him. Maybe he's caught up in the regal attitude that the Krampus costume demands. Either way, we walk into the cold early evening, our breaths pluming out in front of us. Holiday music plays over the loudspeakers, and at least two people dressed in choir robes walk by doing scales and making strange throat sounds as they warm up their voices.

Harry sniffs the air. "The weather is turning afoul. Snow is destined to fall." He looks wistfully up into the night's sky as if he hopes it will start dumping piles of the stuff.

My weather app agrees: Flurries are expected throughout the night. "Great. This is going to be so much fun," I say through gritted teeth. I prefer the fall. The weather is always either blustery with leaves floating about or warm and crystal clear. Add in Halloween, and you have the perfect time of year. Frozen is not my thing.

Visions of singing off-key with my group, shaking from the freezing temperature, and people booing at us fill my thoughts. I stare after a cheerful group of people that brush past us. I don't remember ever being that happy.

"We could look for him on the way to our Figgy Pudding spot, where the crew waits for us."

Harry nods. "Good."

"I think our spot is that way." I point in the direction of the group who just went by.

Harry pulls me along with the flow of the crowd, and I reach up to link arms with him. It's funny how out here, no one even notices he looks different than everyone else. There are no screams, no one trying to back away. One person even stops us and asks for a selfie with him. Out here, you can be anyone you want to be. I spare another glance at my phone to read the messages in more depth. Scrolling through them, I notice that not a single message is from Harry telling us he'd be late.

"Hey." I elbow him to get his attention.

He looks down at me. "Hey."

"Why didn't you answer any of the texts or messages we sent you?"

He shakes his head, eyes narrowed. "You attempted to reach me?"

I nod. "For two days. Where's your phone?" I ask, tilting my head.

"I don't use modern contraptions. They just get in the way."

"Since when? You just messaged me for a booty call not two nights ago." We stop to let a little kid dash by to his mom, waiting on the other side.

"I don't know of this booty call you speak of." He frowns.

"Ugh! Are you serious?" Why does he have to be so sexy and maddening all at the same time?

"I have upset you, my lady. I meant no disrespect." His body is warm by my side, and I can swear electricity zaps between us.

I sigh. Is he losing his mind? "Whatever."

He pauses, puts his hand over mine, and we continue strolling along. "I know not of this indiscretion you speak of, but I shall make it up to you."

My head feels better, but my stomach churns, and I'm a little woozy in fear of missing the competition. I try to distract myself by reciting the lyrics to our carols without looking at the song folder shoved in my bag. Karol of the Bells is the first song that comes to mind. I start to sing under my breath to try and keep calm. Harry does his head turning-ear cocking-nose sniffing thing as we go.

His head snaps to the left as he focuses on something in the distance. "The child's scent is strong in the air." He pulls me with him as he walks faster.

An orange head ducks into the coffee shop. What twelve year old's mother would let him have caffeine at five in the evening? Fred's satisfied grin floats into my mind. Will it ever go away?

But that fits.

"Follow me," Harry says. He must have seen him too.

Hope rises in my chest, burning like vomit. We're going to make it back in time for the competition!

I yawn, opening the back of my throat like my vocal coach taught me, and do scales as we walk. The notes are quiet inside my head, but Harry's glance sideways at me proves otherwise. He smiles softly and doesn't say a word, just patiently drags me through the crowded sidewalk.

Encouraged by his smile, I switch to a different key. I might be imagining it, but I can swear that the people walking past are squinting at me in confusion. One child looks at me in outright disgust, covering their ears. And then it hits me. Maybe I don't sound as good out loud as I do inside my head. I snap my mouth closed and stop humming. My cheeks tingle, and my chest constricts as embarrassment floods my body, that hope slowly sinking.

****

The next thing I know, we're standing in front of the coffee shop. Harry pulls the door open and holds it ajar so I can enter first. A wall of bodies prevents us from going too far into the store. The warm smell of freshly brewed coffee wafts toward us seductively. We're stuck at the back of the room. Good thing Harry is so tall.

A *woosh* of cold air from behind us whirls around the entryway.

"There you are," a familiar voice says.

I glance behind me, and there's Cindy. Her nose is red from the cold, her curls back in pristine order. She shoves me aside, my right breast smashing up against an embarrassed-looking teenager. Betcha he never dreamt he'd get to second base at a coffee shop tonight.

I carefully turn around so I'm not pleasuring the teen without consent and forget why we're here. Because Cindy is pressing her chest against Harry, *that look* on her face. I'm not dumb. I've seen how Harry flirts with her at parties and how she responds.

"Have you found Fred?" she asks, her grimace widening. I know that look: that's Cindy's evil grin. She has a million shades of grimaces in her arsenal, but not even one is a kind smile.

"Thought I saw him come in here." I narrow my eyes. *Harry's mine,* I think. "Hey, I have an idea," I say out loud, leaning toward the two. "You should go look somewhere else." *Like Canada.* "We've got this

41

covered."

I can't tell what Harry thinks about Cindy's advances, being I'm only at chest level. I lean back to see his face. Wonder of wonders, he's panning the room in search of the kid as if he's immune to Cindy's feminine wiles. The knot in my stomach loosens a little.

I tap Harry on the arm. "We need to hurry. Do you see Fred?"

The kid I just squished my breasts against looks back at me, shrinking away.

Harry's eyes narrow, and he shakes his head. "No, he's not here."

"Bossing him around?" Cindy asks. "You're sure full of yourself."

I return her glare. "I'm *politely* asking Harry a question." I move forward as space opens up. "That's a lot different from ordering someone around. You should try it sometime."

Cindy stands on tiptoe and whispers in Harry's ear. He leans away from her, his upper lip curled in disgust. "Why do you touch me?"

With a shift of her weight, she giggles and rubs her face against Harry's chest, breathing in before straightening up. "You're silly. I'll meet you back at the space."

What the hell? That bitch is trying to make a move on my man—in front of me. For the love of all that's Christmas, she's married!

Cindy pushes her way through the newcomers to the door. A *swish* and a breeze later, and we're alone in the crowded cafe.

Reeling from Harry's reaction to Cindy, I can't help but smile. He just dissed her. He's never done that before. "Let's go?" I turn as best I can to propel Harry to the exit.

He nods and gently slides past me to open the door, ducking his head to get ready to exit.

Sounds from the street outside sneak through the cracked open door; people talk and laugh, the carol 'We Wish You a Merry Christmas' is on at full volume. Harry pushes harder with shouts of "ouch," and "hey," from the other side. Apparently, he's shoving a group of people jammed up against the door out of the way. A pair of twenty-something hipsters are our victims, one of them rubbing their nose. Who stands with their nose pressed against the entrance of a coffee shop? That's just asking for trouble.

"Sorry about that." I slip through an opening in the crowd, leaving Harry behind. I need a little space to think. What the hell is up with Cindy? Where did the kid go? Am I going to destroy the lyrics and sing off-key, sparking a social media frenzy?

I risk a glance behind me when I make it to the corner, but I can't see Harry anywhere. What if he doesn't make it in time for the performance? I'm shaking; my coat pulled tight around my body. Another wave of dizziness takes over, but I shove it down, taking slow, deep breaths. Harry's an adult. He knows where we're meeting; he can figure it out.

An elf slams into me, and my muscles melt, my body sliding in slow motion to the ground.

Guess you can't shove down dizzy spells.

Chapter 5

We're in the middle of a crowded street corner when we collide. Their boxes fly into the air. The lights sparkle around us, their twinkle turning into blurred dots.

There's a moment where I swear time freezes—like we're in the space between two notes of a song playing over the loudspeaker. The elf's hands shoot out impossibly fast, catching me, somehow grabbing this box and that in our soundless bubble. The elf winks at me, and everything seems to go back to normal, the music blaring and people talking all around us.

"Gosh, I'm sorry," the elf says, helping me to stand. "You need to drink some water." Their hat jingles as they catch the last tumbling boxes with ease. "Easy to get dehydrated in this weather." The elf holds me with their stare until I return their look. "Don't be afraid to change course. It will all work out." They hurry off.

What just happened there? As the people around me stop spinning, I become aware of my surroundings. This looks like the heart of the caroling area, fully packed with booths, carolers, and shoppers. The information booth is to my left: an arrangement of tables under a canopy. There are so many people around me I don't see Harry anywhere. I'm kicking myself for not holding on to him when we left the coffee shop.

I might be imagining things, but it sounds like Marion and June are nearby. Following their voices, I can see them standing in the middle of a group of people at the information booth, their costumes making them stand out.

"Khalie! We found Fred!" Marion calls, her back rigid against the cold. My app says it's dropped to twenty-five degrees.

Anger simmers inside of me as I shove through carolers and people dressed in thick jackets and gloves. "Great," I say, finally making it to the table. I feel like crap, yet I still wasted an hour of my life looking for that kid. I've called in sick to work for less! Never mind the fact that Fred and his mom have taken away my practice time.

"Can I help you?" A slack-jawed woman in a Santa hat and jacket asks.

"I have cookies for the bake sale," I say over the music on the loudspeakers and the people talking around us. "Where should I bring them?" The wind blows through my thin trench coat. I wish I had a warmer coat.

She picks up the paper and points to a letter. "Go over there. See where that person with the Santa hat is sitting?"

"Oh yeah." I nod.

"That's the one."

"Thank you." I turn and leave with June and Marion.

"We're this way," June says, guiding us. A lazy snowflake drifts by.

I reach out to try and catch it, my fingers as cold as popsicles. "Would you look at that? Harry was right."

June stops, forcing the stream of foot traffic to reroute around us amid loud complaints. She tilts her head back, mouth open to try and catch another one, but Marion tugs on us to get us moving.

Our breath forms a cloud around the three of us as we plow our way through the crowded intersection. The realization that the competition is going to happen, whether I'm ready or not, is sinking in. My thoughts turn to Cindy, making my stomach roll. Who does she think she is moving in on my man? I can't stop replaying the way she pressed her face into Harry's chest and whispered in his ear at the coffee shop.

"Are we close?" My nose is numb.

June nods. "Yes." She points through the packed street up ahead.

"Who are those people talking to Dina and Fred?" A surge of adrenaline shoots to my icy toes. A string bean man and a short woman with spiky grey hair hold out a donation jar to them.

"That's the gal running the whole thing." Marion speeds up.

My insides seize up. "They're judges?" My voice squeaks on the last syllable. It's like I'm in high school trying to get the choir leader's approval all over again.

I walk faster.

"Yes, I think they're half of the team that judges," June says.

They are walking to the next group when we arrive. June goes to her bag resting at Harry's feet. Well shit. So that's where he went.

He's sitting on her cooler, mask off, peering at his phone. He looks like a little boy who just woke from a nap, cheeks rosy, the Krampus costume pooling around him. That's weird. I could swear he was wearing makeup earlier. What's that about? The flaccid mask and taloned gloves that lay on his lap look even more disturbing than when he wore them.

"Khalie! Where on earth did you go?" I turn, and there's Cindy, with Dina and Fred to her left. A guy and two girls walk up and start talking to June. I crane to hear what they're saying, but there is too much going on around us.

"We kept texting you saying Harry found Fred, but you never answered," Dina says as loud as she can. Is it me, or does she say everything in a snotty voice?

June's laughter catches my attention. She's saying something about our ghost hunting group.

A kid dashes past me, bumping into everyone they go by as I pull my phone out. I scowl and look at the chat. Sure enough, there are twenty-two missed group messages, all coming in about the time we left the coffee shop. "Sorry, I've been trying not to use my phone to save battery." I mean, partial truth, I *do* need to save my battery.

Marion adjusts her chignon and sighs. "We need to work on our communication."

"Hey Harry." I wave at him.

"Hey." His face is slack with disinterest. Music wafts up; he's watching videos for the songs we're going to sing tonight.

Oh God, he didn't practice already? For the past month, our group got together twice a week to practice our songs. By now, we have the harmony nailed, but he hadn't made it to any practices.

Fred crouches on the ground playing with an old handheld video game, long coat wrapped around his thighs. I flick his ear. "Where have you been? I can't believe I wasted an hour looking for you even though you set me on fire. I should have called the cops."

It looks like he's trying to melt into the ground.

47

Maybe he feels terrible about maiming me and ruining my costume.

"I didn't do it." He's absorbed in his game.

Yeah, maybe not. The trio walks off, leaving the seven of us alone in the middle of the crowded intersection.

Cindy puts an arm around Harry, rubbing his short brown hair. She calls out to me, "Harry was stuck in traffic when we were trying to reach him. He found the kid on his way over here." Her voice is loud and clear over the murmur of conversation and music.

She's not even trying to hide that she's interested in him anymore, that wench.

I go to Harry's other side and grab his arm to get his attention. "Stuck in traffic? Nice excuse, dude."

June snorts as she looks down at the lyrics in her hands.

"What do you mean?" he asks, finally making eye contact with me. He's pale as fuck, accent gone.

"I've been trying to reach you since last night." I swat at his phone. "Then you show up here and lie to me about not having a cell phone?" Harry shrinks away. To Cindy, I say, "He was helping me look for Harry most of this time. How was he stuck in traffic *then*?"

She looks up to the left, confusion pulling her mouth into a frown.

"I never lied about not having a cell phone." He gives me his innocent puppy dog look.

"Yeah, sure." I let out a sigh. "Are we still getting dinner after?"

"Eh, we'll see." He turns back to Cindy with a wink. She fluffs her curls as he nuzzles his face into her side, tugging her down. He whispers into her ear, and she blushes, looking at him under her lashes with a grimace, her version of coy. Gross.

I start to ask him why he ditched me after the coffee shop, ready to spit out something that might make him mad but change my mind. I mean, we spent the better part of the last hour searching for Fred together. He'd shared some private things about his dad. That means that he might be ready for the next step in our relationship. You know, changing social media statuses and telling our friends that we're together. He's probably just giving into Cindy because it's easier to hide our relationship until we go public.

Harry rises and shoves past me to get to June, who is people watching. "Hey lady, can I have a songbook? I don't know the lyrics to our carols." He gives her an awkward side-hug.

June shrinks away from his touch and smiles. "Sure. Here you go." A flicker of doubt passes over her features.

"June needs one too, dufus." I bop him on the arm. Harry gives me a who cares shrug.

Another group of people walk up and start quizzing her.

Marion's voice carries over everyone's head. "I have a spare! June, take mine."

I look down at Harry's legs as they talk, noticing he's not as tall as he was earlier. He must have gotten tired of wearing the stilts. Understandable. They would be hard to walk on, especially after we'd been running all over the mall.

June answers the group's questions and ends up getting a tip for the donation jar.

My eyes wander to the melted patch of fur next to Harry's tail from when Cindy put out the fire. I'm not sure why he changed into the old costume, but that's hardly a bad thing.

Fred squats next to his mom, flicking another lighter. I lean down and snatch it from him.

"Where did you guys find Fred?" I put my bag of cookies down.

"He was at the cookie table."

"I told them I lost my mommy, and they gave me cookies." Fred grins.

"Why didn't you answer any of our texts?" Marion crouches next to him.

I'm listening to their conversation with one ear, but most of my attention is on Harry and Cindy.

Fred tugs on my skirt. "Where's the Krampus that's been following me?"

I look down at him and scowl, pulling my skirt out of his grubby little hand. "He's right here. What are you talking about?"

"That's not the same guy from the garage."

I shove the kid aside with my leg as he grabs at my skirts again. "Sure, it is. Who else would it be?"

"The other guy is nicer."

"Nice isn't Khalie's type."

"Shut up, Dina." I turn my back with a swish of my charred skirt.

Another group walks up to us. June smiles at them and says quietly to us, "Come on, let's try to get along." She turns back to help them.

"Don't be a pest, Fred. How can there be more than one Krampus?" Marion asks.

"She's right. There can't be two Krampuses," Cindy says.

My mind spins, thinking about the past hour.

There's that time when Harry caught me when I stumbled in the garage. We had that sweet conversation about our dads at the bookstore, and he always opened doors for me. He even complimented my voice and asked me what I thought about things. It did feel like a new and improved Harry. He had me falling for him all over again, despite his shortcomings. People change, right? It's not *that* unbelievable.

"June," I say, getting her attention. "I'm going for a walk to clear my head, okay?"

"Good idea. Take a breather. Grab a hot chocolate or something."

I nod and turn on my heel.

****

I walk through the crowded intersection, staring at the ground. Someone grabs my arm. When I look up, my heart skips a beat.

Cindy tugs me out of the path of foot traffic. "What's going on between you and Harry?"

"What are you talking about?"

Back at our spot, Harry has his mask and gloves back on, waving at little kids walking by. Seeing him pose for pictures in full costume niggles at my brain. *What is it?*

"Oh, c'mon, you know what I'm talking about. Good ole Krampus over there." She gestures to the sexy beast that is Harry.

A baby in a stroller looks up at him and starts screaming, their little mouth wide open, tears streaming down their reddened face. Their mom pushes the stroller away, shooting Harry an angry glance. I start to laugh. "Oh, Harry. Yeah. He's all right. We hang out once in a while. No big deal."

Cindy raises her eyebrow, her porcelain skin luminous in the gentle evening light. "You're sleeping with him, aren't you?"

"Nah. I wish." Harry doesn't want anyone to know about us. Made me promise that I'd never tell anyone. Besides, there isn't a whole lot of sleeping going on when we get together.

"You're lying. I can tell." Cindy leans in, her turquoise eyes boring holes into me.

I shake her off. "What's up with the third degree?" Seriously, I'll work a whole month of overtime to get her on a bus to Canada if it means she's out of my life.

"Ladies, let's leave this for later." June walks up to us. "We're here as representatives of The NIGHT Crew. We need to be professional."

"Sure." Cindy gives her the side-eye. To me, she says, "We're not done with this conversation," and sways off in Harry's direction.

"She's just jealous." June and I watch her walk up to Harry. The look on Cindy's face morphs into her version of a warm smile. Yeah, another shade of grimace.

"But she's married."

"And?" June says. "You ever see that stop someone before?"

"Um, lots of people."

"She's just lonely. Her husband is never home. Don't worry. She would never do anything about it. It's harmless."

From where we're standing, I see Harry rooting around in my bag. I push past June and start running. He comes up with the dollar store box full of my cookies, and I watch in horror as he takes the lid off and pulls out a handful. He tilts back the mask and raises a kolache to his lips. My heart starts to pound. That selfish asshole!

"Stop!" I scream, holding my skirts in my hands and leaping the last three feet to his side.

It makes no difference. By the time I've crossed the gap between us, Harry's not only chomping away on another cookie, but he's holding out the box for others to take one as well.

"You have no right to eat those cookies. I baked them using my oma's special recipe to donate to the charity booth over there. Stop eating them, *now*!" I yank the box out of his hands. There are maybe seven cookies gone by now.

"What kind of cookies are these? They're delicious."

I sigh, snapping the lid on with a click. "They're Apricot Kolaches." I'm so done with him. And to think I was just falling back in love with him, even getting ready to buy him dinner, and ask him to be my boyfriend.

"They're so flakey. Wow, you've got mad baking skills." Crumbs spray out of Harry's mouth as he speaks. I should be flattered, but this is the last straw.

"You should ask before you start eating other people's food."

"What's the big deal?"

"What's the big deal?" My voice is so high it doesn't even sound like mine. "They're not yours!" Is he really that selfish?

I'm just done. This is my moment to shine, and I can see it slipping away. I wanted to prove that all the hard work I put in perfecting my warble, all that money mom threw away on voice lessons when I was a teenager, would finally pay off.

Angrily, I stuff what's left of the Kolaches into my bag. "I'm going to drop the cookies off at the cookie booth."

"Good idea," Marion says.

"I'm sorry that happened, Khalie. He didn't know you made them special for the bake sale," June says, trying to smooth things over.

"It's fine." I don't want to take my anger out on her.

"No hurry." Dina shoves greasy hair behind her ear. "That short woman with the spikey hair said we've got some time. They don't start with the caroling until six thirty."

I nod, my body flooding with adrenaline. Funny how it clears your head.

"Be back in a half-hour," someone yells to my back. Probably Marion again. She's so bossy. I wave my hand at them to let them know I'd heard and stomp off.

Chapter 6

It's gotten colder, with more snowflakes spinning in the air. I pass someone dressed as Santa, ho-ho-ho-ing and waving at the crowd. "Hi Khalie," he says.

I stop and look at him. "Do I know you?"

"So good to see you all grown up."

Now, that's just creepy. "Uh, I knew you when I was a kid?"

He laughs, holding his jiggling belly. "You could say I've known you since you were born." He winks. His costume is way better than everyone else's tonight. And then I remember the elf from earlier. Both of them look great.

"Oh, I'm sorry. I don't recognize you. What's your name?"

He laughs again. "Santa to the kids, but since you're all grown up now, you can call me Kris."

I wrack my brain for someone named Kris and come up blank. Probably one of my stepdad's old friends. "Oh, uh. Nice to see you again."

A bum dressed in grungy oversized clothes stumbles past us, the ripe aroma of pee and alcohol singeing my nostrils. "Spare some change?" He holds his fingerless-gloved hand out, palm up.

"Do I look like a bank?" I pull back.

"Fuck you." The rank man tugs his grey skull cap down and wanders off.

Santa watches the whole exchange, a perplexed look on his face. "Khalie, it wouldn't hurt to try kindness for a change. You never know how close you are to being out on the streets yourself."

I ponder his words, thinking how I'd gone from renting my own one-bedroom apartment to moving into a studio. After a stint of sleeping on other people's couches, I'm now renting a room in a cranky old cat-ladies house. He's not wrong.

"I'm sorry. I just feel awful, and I'm having a terrible day, and I have to get these cookies to the bake sale booth." Tears burn my eyes. "And I'm supposed to sing in the caroling competition, but I don't think I'm welcome there anymore."

The dam breaks, and I'm ugly crying now, the tears freezing before they get even halfway down my face.

"Hey, hey, hey. It will all work out. Just you wait and see." Santa pats my shoulder.

His costume is exactly what I imagine Santa would wear if he were real. Maybe Santa and the elf are from the same talent agency.

"Thank you. I appreciate your kindness. But I need to go." I turn to continue my journey. "Merry Christmas," I call out and walk away to his 'Ho ho ho Merry Christmas' calling after me.

A siren blips at the end of the street about two blocks away. The crowd seems to be migrating in that direction, clearing a path for me in the swirling snow. What the heck is going on? I continue to the cookie booth, pushing in front of a rag-tag line of people, waiting their turn to buy cookies and cocoa.

A dumpy-looking woman wearing a Santa hat and glued on elf ears stares at me, brows knit together. The skinny man I'd seen earlier making rounds to all the singing groups sits next to her.

It's her left ear, the glue dried in crusty chunks on her jaw that I'm staring at when I start to talk. "Excuse me. I'm dropping off cookies."

The woman looks up and points to the end of the line. "Sorry ma'am, you'll need to stand in line. First come, first serve!"

"Did you hear what I just said? I'm dropping off cookies for you to sell." My words are slow and concise.

"Oh, I heard you okay. Go to the back of the line, and I'll help you when it's your turn."

"But," I begin to say.

"Back of the line." She gestures her pointing finger twice to show the path she wants me to take.

"Fine." I stomp off to the back of the line, shoving past the stupid people wasting my time. Man, that woman is cranky. She's going to make me miss the competition. Who cares if I'm not welcome; I'm not going to let the Harry-Cindy business and that little shit Fred ruin my night.

About seven minutes later, enough time for my headache to come back full force and that strange underwater feeling to come back, it's my turn. The cranky woman says, "What can I get for you today?" as if we'd never talked at all.

I pull out my box of cookies and drop them on the table. "Here you go. The NIGHT Crew's contribution."

She pulls out a sheet of paper and plops it in front of me. "Did you fill out one of these yet?"

"I'm sorry I forgot." I pull out the completed form from my bag.

"Perfect." She roots under the table for another

clipboard with a handful of papers on it. "Go ahead and print your name right here." She points with a ballpoint pen, "and sign here, and put the time there."

I lean forward and scribble what she asks for, wishing I could just lie down and take a nap.

"Are you having a good night?" she asks.

I want to laugh. Does she not remember I was just here? "Oh yeah, great." I yawn and straighten up, shouldering my bag.

"Good! You didn't have any problems with that monster walking around, did you?"

This stops me in my tracks. "Monster?"

"Yeah, tall guy in a furry brown costume, horns, wicker basket." She gestures horns with her fingers for effect.

"Um, no one like that is bothering me." I back up. What kind of trouble has Harry gotten himself into? "Is that why the cops are here?"

"Oh yeah, someone from the sandwich store called them. Scared off all their customers, the manager said."

Oh, dear. "Gee, that's terrible. I haven't seen him." I clear my throat. "Sorry, gotta go." I turn and power walk back to our spot.

Do I tell Harry the cops are after him? Should we hide him? What if he gets arrested? I break into a half jog, working myself into a frenzy.

If he gets arrested, we won't be able to perform. They'll probably just kick us out of the competition, right? A hugely pregnant woman waddles against the grain of the oncoming foot traffic, stopping me short. My heart slams in my chest, making my head hurt even worse. I change course and dash around her. This has to be the worst night of my life. Harry will get arrested, and we're not going to be able to compete, and it's all that little shit's fault. Fuck Dina. Fuck Freddy.

No, wait a minute. Figgy Pudding is a big deal. I can't let them take this away from me. We can sing without Harry; we've been practicing without him for a month.

I'm so close I can see people stopping in front of our group, asking questions, and tossing money into the Figgy Pudding donation bucket.

Harry is waving like one of those mechanized toys, letting everyone else do the talking. It would be hard to talk in a mask anyway. Just the sight of him and I can feel the connection we'd formed earlier today vibrating through me, dampening my headache. We can't let him get arrested. He's, like, the reason for the season. We need him here to help us pull this off.

I run over to my group and do the only thing I can think of to keep Harry from getting arrested.

****

Everyone is quiet, looking over the lyrics when I trot up to them. "Hey, June," I call out. "Can I talk to you in private? I think you might want to hear this."

"Sure, sounds good." She turns her back to the group. "Go ahead?"

Something about the way she's standing and the looks on the other's faces raises my hackles. "Did I miss something?"

"Nothing exciting going on here." She angles her body so I can't see the rest of the group. I try to look around her, but she shifts with me. June isn't a tiny thing, now add in her giant hat and voluminous clothing, and she's doing a fine job of preventing me from seeing what's going on behind her.

"I wanted to say this in private, but whatever. Did you hear that the police are here? Someone at the cookie booth asked me if the monster had been bugging me."

June's mouth drops open, and she turns around. "You don't think they're talking about Harry, do you? I mean, he's been here the whole time."

"There are two Krampuses. I told you. Why doesn't anyone listen to me?" Fred whines.

Dina kicks at him. "You're in trouble, mister. Shut it."

"What did he do now?" I duck and twist around them to try and see what they're hiding.

Cindy and Harry are up close to each other, Harry's hand under Cindy's chin, their lips locked together. My stomach gurgles in protest.

I lunge on them, circling Cindy's neck with my hands, yelling, "Noooo! He's mine!"

Cindy starts to scream in a strained voice, scratching at me. "Get off of me!"

"What the hell are you doing?" Harry yanks me off Cindy, his eyes wild. "Khalie's crazy. Someone help me here."

"I'm not crazy. You're a lazy, cheating asshole!" I'm panting, his grip on my arms so tight it hurts.

June pulls me out of Harry's hands. "She's got a point, Harry."

Cindy sputters and rubs her neck, scooting to a sitting position.

"Khalie, I don't know what you're talking about." He puts his hands behind his back and looks at his feet. "I am not yours. I'm single. I don't know where you got that idea."

"Gee, I don't know. Maybe a year of sleeping with

you?" That's when that string bean guy jogs up.

"Time to start, everyone." He claps his hands, a broad smile on his face.

"Great, thanks." June turns and glares at everyone before looking back at him.

We watch him lope off to the next group.

June clammers to get the old-fashioned boom box positioned so Fred can hit the on/off buttons. "Okay, everyone, in your places." She puts her hand on my shoulder. "Except for you. I want you to go take a breather. It's not healthy for you here."

A storm is whistling and banging around in my chest, tearing down all the hopes, dreams and lies I'd carefully constructed. "Okay," I say in a small voice.

June hands me a bottle of water. "Drink some water. Find a bathroom and get cleaned up." She rubs my shoulder.

I want to cry and yell and scream that it's not fair. I've waited all year for this, and now my asshole ex-boyfriend and his hussy are taking it away from me?

Harry is helping Cindy stand, a protective arm around her waist. My chest expands in grief with each heartbeat.

Cindy catches my eye and waves at me, triumph making her eyes twinkle, her mouth curve into…is that a smile? The first one I've ever seen on her. I take one step in her direction, white noise filling my ears— another step. And then I remember plan A.

"Here's the monster the cops are looking for!" I yell out, bouncing in excitement. "Someone get the cops!"

June shakes her head and turns her back to me. She points down the street. "Just go."

All around us, people break into song. At least three

Christmas carols are simultaneously being sung, so June queues Fred to turn on the boom box. "And one, two, three," she instructs, and my group erupts into "We Wish You a Scary Christmas."

Off in the distance, footsteps thud toward us. I stay put, refusing to miss the moment Harry is hauled away for his misdeeds.

A woman cop jogs up. "Did you say there's been a monster sighting?"

I turn around and point at Harry in his Krampus costume.

"I'm sorry, where?" She looks past Harry.

"That's him, right there." Then I register what was bugging me about Harry's costume.

"No, that's a man in a bad costume. We're looking for *him*." She holds up her phone. A picture of the tall, muscular man I'd spent an hour looking for Fred with is displayed there.

"Oh," is all I can think to say. It's obvious they're not the same person. Why didn't I see it sooner?

The cop puts her hand to her ear; her finger held up in a wait gesture as she listens to something. "Gotta run," she says, and she's gone, blonde ponytail bouncing.

My heart sinks. Tingles that have nothing to do with the temperature flood my chest. On the one hand, that means I met someone who loves the monster I've been reading about all these years as much as I do. He has to for all the attention he put into getting the costume just right. And he's sexy as hell. On the other, my ghost hunting group just gave me the cold shoulder, taking away my dream of singing in a choir.

Can I just die now?

So much for plan A.

Chapter 7

June scowls at me and points again, and I get the message. With my backpack and bag in hand, I stalk off.

I wander through the festive streets, sliding between people who don't even seem to notice I'm there. I'm invisible here, just like I am to stupid Harry. I walk until my feet ache from the cold, not looking at anyone or anything. A bench appears in my line of sight, and miracle of all miracles, it's empty.

Tentatively I open the bottle of water June gave me. My head isn't any better, and my mouth and throat are so dry. I'm flat out of headache medicine, but everyone might be right. Water could help. I'm not seated five minutes before someone plops down next to me. The scent of piss and alcohol finds me before I even look up: Yup, it's the bum again, his trousers hanging so low on his skinny hips I can see his grimy once-white underwear.

"Down on your luck?" His hands are gripping a giant sized coffee cup.

"You could say that."

He holds the cup of coffee out to me in an unsteady hand, steam rising from the sipping hole on top. "Here, you can have this."

I know he's reading my expression by his next words. "Don't worry. I haven't had any yet." He pauses, tilts his head, and then changes his tune. "Well, I opened it and dumped out some coffee. Some guy gave me a brand-new bottle of cognac, so I filled half of the cup up with that." His hand trembles as he holds it out to me, the most earnest look on his face.

I lean down and sniff, the vapors making my nose tingle. On second thought, "Yes, thank you. I'd love some."

Here is this man so much worse off than me, offering me an expensive cup of free brandy coffee. It would be worse than rude to say no.

"Want to talk about it?" He shoves his hands under his thighs.

"It's complicated." I take a sip, the warmth from the brandy shooting fire down my throat, the coffee itself cooled by the alcohol. And yet still, it helps. "This is good."

He smiles and sits back. His shoulders are slumped forward, his knees pressed together. "It's good to try something new once in a while."

My whole night has been insane. From the moment Dina and Fred got in the car, all the way to now. "It seems today is the day for that." I hold out the coffee to him. "Want to share?"

He looks relieved, smiles, and takes the cup back, removing the lid to take a long swallow. The shaking in his hands lessens by the time he hands back the cup. "Thank you." Even his voice is stronger.

"Welcome." And then I launch into the story of Harry and Khalie. How I was so in love with him, all the way up to him breaking up with me in front of everyone. I don't leave out a single thing. I have to hand it to the man: he nods and takes back the cup every time I pass it to him, always returning it to me.

I'd never dreamed I'd spend my night with the homeless folks of downtown Seattle. "Maybe the Universe is trying to tell me something."

"It has a way of doing that," he says. "That man— Harry, was it? You were just comfortable with him. He's not good for you. You know that, right?"

I'm lost in thought, letting his words sink in. "I mean, I think I do? But he's so sexy." I'm remembering our quickies in my bedroom, in the backseat of my car, even in an alley one time. These memories are mixed up with images of the man I'd searched for the kid with this afternoon; his kindness, the addictive smell of his cologne.

The picture the cop had shown me comes to mind. "Or maybe I'm insane." I'm mourning the loss of a relationship with a man who was never good to me. What am I thinking?

"Eh, happens to the best of us." The homeless guy bumps elbows with me.

"And now I'm missing the caroling because I let myself get out of control."

"Why don't you go find Krampus? I bet he'll make you feel better."

I groan. "I know this is confusing, but Harry *is* Krampus. And he's the one who broke up with me." Even as I say the words, I know I need to let that myth go.

The bum guy shakes his head. "No, not the cheater. I'm talking about the real Krampus."

The alcohol must have gone straight to his head. Because even though they are two different people, the Krampus I'd spent time with today isn't a real monster. Person? Yes. Anyhow, that picture proved that Fred wasn't lying. There really are two men dressed as Krampus tonight.

"Well, it's time for me to go. I need to charge my phone."

He nods and points to the burrito place down the street. "If you sit by the window, they have USB charging stations. Got a cable?"

I fish in my bag, and thankfully I'd remembered to bring that at least. I hold it up. "I'm good. Thank you so much for," I gesture to the cup he's holding, taking in our conversation, "everything."

"No problem. It's good to get outside of your comfort zone once in a while. Thanks for the conversation."

I smile and walk past him toward the restaurant he talked about, calling out "Merry Christmas" to him as I go.

"Merry Christmas." He salutes me.

****

There's one space left at the window next to a charging station. I dump my stuff and shuffle through my bag for the cable that I'd just found. Once I've got it plugged in and my phone is charging, I feel a whole lot better about the situation. Or maybe that's the brandy talking. Whatever. I'm warm now, inside and out. My heart might be broken, but I'm not the one standing outside in the snow, singing with ungrateful people.

That and the kind homeless man from earlier this evening is still out there. Sounds like I'm on the winning end of this story.

"Excuse me, Miss? Our seats are for paying customers only." A sinking sensation trickles from my breastbone and travels down to my legs.

I turn to the pimply teenager and try to smile. "Look, I'm having a horrible day. I just got dumped. My phone needs a charge. I have to wait for my group to finish caroling, and I'm low on cash. Can't you help a girl out by letting her stay warm and charge her phone for a half-hour or so?"

He points to the sticker on the window, two seats down, shaking his head. "Sorry, our seats are for paying customers."

Santa strolls past the window we're in front of, a content smile on his jovial face.

I'm hungry anyway. "Fine." I sigh. "Keep an eye on my stuff?"

"Sorry, I have to get back to work." He walks away pushing a mop in a rolling bucket.

"I'll watch your stuff for you," someone says. I turn to see a blond man with a silver puffer coat on.

"Are you sure?" I look around to see if I have another option. Everyone is avoiding eye contact with me. My reflection in the window is that of a woman in terrible makeup and a trashed thrift store costume. I wouldn't help me either.

"Yeah, sure, it's fine," he says.

I smile. It's good to try new things, I tell myself. Like trusting strangers. "Okay, thanks. I'll be right back."

He nods, and I head to the counter. I order, dumping my last crumpled bill and some loose change on the counter in exchange for an empty cup and a burrito. I get eleven cents back, which I pocket, and then head back to my stuff.

Only, nothing is there. The silver guy is gone. My bags are gone. My phone is gone.

A keen wailing fills the air, getting louder by the minute. I know it's coming out of my mouth, but there's nothing I can do to stop it.

"Are you okay, Miss?" A tiny old lady looks up at me with giant brown eyes, her hand on my elbow.

"Ma'am, I'm sorry. We can't have you bothering our customers," some guy says to me.

I whip around and look at him, pulling myself together. It's the same pimply little jerk who got my shit stolen. "It's *you*." I stab my finger into his chest. "You're the one who got my stuff stolen. This is all your fault."

His hands go up in surrender. "I don't know what you're talking about, lady. We have signs up that say you are responsible for your own valuables. This is on you."

"You're the mother fucker who told me I had to buy a damned burrito if I wanted to not freeze to death outside in the snow. And then you wouldn't watch my stuff while I did what you told me to do. That's on *you*." I'm hyperventilating, hands to knees, the room growing smaller as I stand here.

Someone wearing too long black chinos and cheap-looking black tennis shoes walks toward us, hitching up his pants. "Arnold, what's going on here?"

"Don't you start with me too." I straighten up and try to get my breathing under control. The room spins.

"Sir, this woman is disturbing our customers."

I check the new guy's name tag and note that Steve-the-Manager is now in front of me. "Your employee seems to be in cahoots with the local street life. Made me leave my stuff to order a burrito if I wanted to be in here. My stuff got stolen while I was at the counter because of your incompetent Arnold there."

Arnold's cheeks are bright red, his eyes wide in fear.

Steve-the-Manager looks slowly from Arnold to where I'm pointing. "The charging cable is still there, though. M'kay? That's something."

There's that wind again, riling up in my chest. I tilt my head back and scream at the top of my lungs. What did I do to deserve such a shitty day?

All around me, people watch with various expressions on their faces, from outright ambivalence to terror and every shade in between. The terrified ones cling to their belongings as if I'm the one who stole my stuff instead of that shitty silver guy.

"Miss." The manager-guy puts his hand on my shoulder. I don't respond. I can't. I'm this close to— "Excuse me, Miss. I'm sorry, but you'll have to leave. You're upsetting the customers."

My vision closes off to a tiny dot, and there's a chance someone has turned up the heat because sweat drips down my ribcage. I try to stop the sounds coming out of my mouth, but…

The next thing I know, I'm looking up into a jolly face with red cheeks and fluffy white beard and hair. My head pounds as I struggle to sit. There he is, crouched with his hands on his belly, the smile gone from his face. "Ho ho ho. Khalie, what's going on here?"

Our surrounding fades away as I dump out my woes for the second time tonight to a stranger. From the Krampus costume to Harry cheating on me and not singing in the competition. At some point, I notice that the crowd is gathered around us, nodding and getting into my story. Shocked sighs and gasps highlight just what a crappy day I'm having.

"So I tried something new, just like everyone keeps telling me, and look where it got me." I lean into Santa's chest.

Santa helps me stand, takes the burrito I'd purchased from the manager, and guides me out of the store, his arm holding me up.

Snow and clouds of our breath dance around us as we make our way into the night. He guides me to a bench. "Let's sit."

When we're both settled, he says, "It's important to try new things, but sometimes things don't work out the way we want. They turn out the way we need." He pulls a flask out of his waistband, unscrews the lid, and holds it out to me. "Here, have some of this."

First, a homeless guy tries to get me drunk, now Santa. What's going on with this world? But I reach out for it anyway. "What is it?"

"Peppermint hot-cocoa."

How on-theme of him. "Thank you."

I take the flask, wipe the rim and take a sip. It's got a kick to it, but not necessarily alcoholic. "What's that…taste?"

"A little bit of magic goes a long way." He accepts the flask back, secures the lid, and tucks it into his waistband.

"Define magic."

"Industry secret." He smiles. "It's time for you to find Krampus and get everything cleared up."

"You too?" I lean away to look at him. "The homeless guy said the same thing."

Santa takes my hand and waits for me to look him in the eye. "You need to find the real Krampus."

"Why are you pushing him on me so hard? What's it to you?"

He lets go of my hand, his gaze wandering off into

the distance.

"Krampus is my best friend. We've worked together since time before time, and tonight is the happiest I've ever seen him. He hates his job. Hates having to enforce the naughty list. So it's understandable he's grumpy all the time. But not tonight. Tonight, he told me he met the most amazing woman with the face of a goddess."

Me? A goddess? I can't help but laugh. "You tell a good story. Thanks for trying to get my mind off things."

"I'm serious," he says. "Go find Krampus."

And he gets up and walks away, leaving me with my mouth hanging open.

Chapter 8

The snow is coming down heavy, and the trees and planting beds around me bend under the weight of the white fluff. Snow covers some of the Christmas lights; others appear artfully displayed. Despite the magical scenery, tears try to roll down my face. I've calmed down since my episode at the burrito place. Still, there's a burning down deep in my stomach that has nothing to do with the cognac or the magical potion Santa gave me. I need to do something to make my evening better.

As if I summoned it, a familiar voice shouts, "Hey, put me down." Stifled words that I can't quite hear, and then, "Mom. *Mom.* They're touching me! Strangers are touching me!"

Fred is nearby? I jump up and stalk toward the angry pleas coming from the little shit that saw right through Krampus/Harry. I almost feel like I owe him something. I'm running now, pretty sure the kid's at the cookie booth with my apricot kolaches. I need to pick them up anyway. When I get there, a man restrains Fred with one arm, trying to keep him from running away. He is stabbing numbers into his phone with his other hand. A burnt, plasticky smell laces the air, and the steam from a little portable heater fills the space around them.

"Khalie, help. This man is hurting me."

Ignoring the child, I turn to the man. "Excuse me, what's going on here?" I push my shoulders back, trying to look responsible.

"This kid stole cookies." Fred bats at the man's phone, but his captor just gives him a good squeeze putting an end to that. "At first, we didn't care, but when he started hiding under the table and—"

"Well, you know, kids will be kids." I reach for Fred.

"Are you his mother?"

I freeze. "Um, no, but we drove here together. And I know where his mother is."

"I'm sorry. We can only release him to his parents."

I clear my throat. "Come on. He just stole cookies. That's not *that* big of a deal. You can let him go. His mom doesn't need to know about it. She's busy caroling."

"He lit my skirt on fire!" The lady spits out the words, her face smeared in eyeliner, her left rubber ear hanging on by a thread of goo. It kinda looks like that artist guy's self-portrait.

I tilt my head and nod. "Oh yeah, he did that to me too."

"It caught the tent on fire." The man's face is almost purple.

I pull in a cold breath through my teeth, grimacing. "Sorry." How is one child so evil?

"He tied my leg to my chair with a shoelace," someone else says.

Fred stops hollering long enough to smile in satisfaction, then goes back to it. Got to admit, this kid has spunk.

"Why are you hanging around this booth? Why not another one?" I ask him. He's barely dressed for the weather, and he's not even shaking. Maybe he's a demon. I've met an elf and Santa tonight; why is it so far-fetched that this kid is actually a demon?

"No one else would let me hang around."

"And you can't hang around here. You need to be with your mom." I turn to the man. "Let me take him off your hands. I promise to take him back to his mom."

The guy looks between the two ladies behind the tables and me. They nod at him in encouragement. They definitely have had enough of the kid. "Okay. But if there are any more problems with him, we're going to call the cops."

"Fair." I hold up my hands in a peace offering. "And the kolaches are mine. I'm going to grab the container now before we head back."

The woman with the artist's ear hurries to close up the dollar store container and holds it out to me, a pitying look on her face. Not a single cookie is missing. "No one knew what kolaches were."

Seriously? "Um, they're the best cookies in the world." I grab the container from her and drag the kid away by the ear down the street.

"Ow, let go of me."

"Not after how you've been acting."

"This is child abuse."

"Ha. I could have had you thrown in juvie for setting my skirt on fire."

We're awkward as we walk down the middle of the street, passing by groups of people singing Christmas carols. Some are dancing in complicated formations, but most are standing still as they deliver their perfectly modulated notes, practically vibrating from the below-freezing temperature. People stand in front of them with clipboards, smiling as they nod and take notes. I'm trying as hard as I can not to let pangs of jealously take over. Instead, I'm using it to give me the strength to tow this little juvenile delinquent back to his mother.

I can see our group, with Harry-the-ex in the middle, maybe five hundred feet away. It looks like they're cleaning up their stuff. That's when someone behind us starts screaming like a whole litter of dead baby squirrels just fell on their bare feet.

****

I look around, but I know what I'm going to see.

Harry—er—nice Krampus *clip-clops* down the street like a mustang on crack, shoving people aside, snowflakes parting for him. In his wake, people struggle to stand and shake off the collision. We lock eyes, and Santa's words float back to me. *Go find the real Krampus. I've never seen him this happy before.* I turn around to our group and see the real Harry.

"Woah!" Harry's voice is muffled from the mask. "There are two of me." It's like he can read my thoughts. I'm glad he can't, though, because the closer nice Krampus gets, his muscles rippling, his smell preceding him, the weaker I get.

More people scream and run away from the giant furry creature.

"Oh great," June mutters. "Two more than we need."

Cindy elbows her and hisses. "June, we can hear you."

June giggles. "Just kidding. You know I don't mean it."

Cindy shoots her a wide-eyed grimace which June returns with a head shake for emphasis.

Meanwhile, the crowd cowers at the giant harry man

standing before us, phones held to document this situation. Personally, after the day I've had, I think I'm ready to go home with him and let him ravage me.

"Where is the child?" he roars. There's that accent, the word 'where' coming out as 'vair.' The fact he might be Krampus makes his accent even sexier.

Oh, that's right. I look down at the red-headed monster.

"Which child are you looking for." Cindy fiddles with a curl. Is she flirting with *my* Krampus now, too? The bitch already has that idiot Harry. Why does she need this one too?

"Him." Krampus points to the kid I'm holding by the ear.

Krampus's arms are long and muscular, the kind every girl, and a few guys too, want wrapped around them. But his face is more authentic-looking than the mask, and his fingernails are claw-like, way more realistic than Harry's costume. It's obvious now that Santa and the homeless guy were right: this Krampus is the real deal. I'm giddy with excitement.

"Me?" Fred uses my lack of attention to disengage from my grip on his ear.

"What do you want with my son?" Dina is almost purring. She pushes her pouty lips out and leans in, taking a deep breath, clearly taken by the sexy beast like the rest of us.

"The child is on the Naughty List." Krampus points at the kid.

Fred crinkles his nose as if it's painful to think. "Huh."

"Excuse me." I push Dina aside, linking arms with favorite Krampus. "You should probably tell her where you're taking the juvenile delinquent." I mean, I could go on for ages about what I read in books, but this is the real deal.

"Juvenile delinquent?" Dina's face goes red. "Did you just call my kid a juvenile delinquent?"

I guess I said that out loud.

"C'mon Dina, let's face it. You let him run wild." Marion crosses her arms.

"He's a free-range kid. It's a parenting style. You guys don't have kids yet. What do you know?"

"Excuse me. I've raised two kids, and neither of them have been arrested—or set anything on fire." That's Cindy the wench.

"Free-range…like chickens?" Harry asks. "You're raising your kid like fucking chickens?"

"I may not be a parent yet," I say. "But I can promise you if my future kid acts anything like little Freddy here, I might just…" I look from face to face of the people in my group, finishing with Krampus. He squints at me, slowly nodding. "Send him away."

"Yeah, send him away to military school," Harry says.

There's a time when Harry's advice was welcome, even wanted. That time has passed. "Just shut up, Harry."

Dina snarls and leaps at me, a primal scream tearing from her mouth. "You don't know anything about anything."

Krampus puts his paw out, holding her away from me.

Dina's uttering garbled words, and her feet are sliding against the iced-over pavement, head pressed against Krampus's paw. Finally, she backs up with a grunt, swiping her knotted hair out of her eyes.

"You're a shitty ghost hunter; you suck at picking men, and *oh my God,*" she screams, a short, breathy sound. "Who the hell did your makeup?"

After that, she spews all kinds of unintelligible things, some more interesting than others. My favorite: "Let's not forget your costume. You look like a harlot who has been murdered for her bad choice in men."

Someone snorts, and I think Marion outright laughs before saying, "So much for being friends with your fellow ghost hunters."

June reaches out and pats me on the shoulder. "Don't listen to her. You're a great ghost hunter."

Cindy bobs her head from left to right, curls bouncing. "Well, at least she's not shitty."

June twists her mouth and nods, considering her words. "Well, Dina's not wrong about the men part."

"Maybe the makeup too." Marion peers at me. I hug the box of cookies, my lip trembling.

"Dina, she's right about Fred. He's out of control," Cindy, the cheating man-stealing bitch says.

"He's definitely not on Santa's Nice List." Harry lights a cigarette.

"Correct," Krampus says.

"You from Indonesia or something?" Harry says. I hit him reflexively, and he rephrases his question. "I mean, like, you don't talk like us. You have an accent. What's up?"

This has crossed my mind. I just hadn't spoken the words out loud. Everyone nods despite themselves.

"Yeah, where *are* you from?" Dina asks through pouty lips.

Krampus pauses. "Down below."

"Australia? Rad!"

June squints. "That doesn't sound like an Australian accent."

"Am I the only one here wondering how we ended up with two Krampuses?" Marion asks.

Another silence falls on our group. Harry's hand shoots up, but either no one sees it or, more likely, no one wants to hear what he has to say. And then everyone is talking all at once.

"I did put out a call to the group to see if anyone wanted to be Krampus."

"Didn't June ask if anyone had a Krampus costume because hers is thrashed?"

"You guys can't honestly believe we're the only one who had this idea," Harry says.

"That's true."

"Yeah."

Once everyone seems to have spoken their mind, Harry speaks up. "Why don't we just ask him. It's not like he can't hear us."

The group grows quiet after Harry's unexpectedly wise words. Soon, everyone nods and turns to where Krampus was standing at my side. But he's gone.

"Where'd he go?" Marion cranes her neck to see around the milling crowd.

The first thing that crosses my mind is to look for Fred. Sure enough, he's no longer standing next to his mom.

"Fred's gone too," I point out.

And we're back where we were when we got here, times two: no Krampus and now, no Fred.

Chapter 9

June and I bat away snowflakes the size of quarters as we scramble to clean up the last of everyone's stuff as fast as we can. Everyone else took off to find the kid. Music plays over speakers down the street where the sing-off for the finalists is going on. A shout comes from the opposite direction, stopping us in our tracks.

"Fred! I found Fred!" It's Dina. She's a street away at the cookie booth. "He's right here!"

Marion is with her, a thunderous look on her face.

I grab my box of cookies and head over, watching the scene unfold. Krampus holds Fred by the ankle, the kid flailing in the air upside down. Fred has bright smudges of red on his cheeks and what looks like chocolate smeared all around his mouth. Damn it. Why does he keep going back to the cookie booth?

Dina stands in between her dangling child and Krampus, trying to push Krampus away from Fred. It's comical, really. Does she realize if she pushes too hard, the kid will fall on his head? I open my mouth to say something but then change my mind. The kid could use a knock or two.

At first, Dina pleads to us in a hysterical voice to help her. I'm having trouble understanding what she's saying, her voice too shrill. Something about Krampus trying to stuff her child into his satchel, just like in the German folklore. From the looks of it, it's not working.

The kid kicks and swings his free arms and one leg in every direction like a cat getting tossed into a bath. He's screaming and yelling, his words barely recognizable over Dina's howling pleas.

What we can hear is pure Fred gold. "I hate you. Don't touch me! He's trying to kidnap me! Let go of me!"

A siren blips; red and blue lights reflect off the windows and snow covering the ground. "Police! Put the child down," a voice on a loudspeaker says.

Fred stops flailing, a slow smile spreading across his face.

Krampus freezes, his eyes wide, ears tilted back. There's a pause where both mother and child go silent, and then the speaker starts again.

"Put the child down and get down on the ground." There's a rustling, plasticky sound as the female cop from earlier pulls her gun out of its holster.

Fred kicks once, twice. Krampus's ears go flat, and he slowly lowers the kid to the ground.

Everyone in the cookie booth is preoccupied with the scene in front of them, mouths hanging open.

The kid takes off at a trot, but no one seems to care. A second cop gets out of his car, gun drawn. "Keep your hands up and lay down on your stomach."

This is really happening. What a fucking day this has been.

No one steps in to help this poor man on his knees, the snow whirling all around us. Not Harry, which I would never have expected. Not June or any of the rest that came with us tonight. Well, probably because, you know, it's the police. Also, partly because the snow is mesmerizing, freezing us into place in more ways than one.

"The handcuffs don't fit around his wrists," the male cop says to the officer with the blonde ponytail standing about two paces behind him.

"Here, use these." She hands him some zip ties.

"Thanks." Cop number one takes them and holds Krampus's wrists together. "You are under arrest for child endangerment and disturbing the peace."

As if.

"Okay, okay, I know he was man-handling a kid, but that wasn't just any kid."

The cop stops writing and looks up at me. "We have a zero-tolerance policy for child abuse here in Seattle."

I can't believe I'm witnessing what may be the love of my life getting arrested. What can I do to get him out of this?

Someone chokes on a laugh behind me, but I ignore them and keep pressing on. "Yeah, here's the thing. He wasn't abusing the kid. It was self-defense."

"Self-defense? How badly could a kid hurt a seven-foot man?"

"Look, sir, I know it sounds like I'm making it up. But that kid set my skirt on fire."

"Me too," the woman with the missing ear says from the cookie booth behind me. "And it caught our tent on fire."

"He bit me," a random guy says. I don't know when Fred decided to chew on them, but at least the rando is speaking out. My own group is staying silent.

The second cop walks up to us, her hands on her hips, a notepad under one hand. "We'll make sure to share this information with the detective." She nods her chin once.

"But wait." My stomach is full of dancing feet. I'm running out of options here.

"I'm sorry, Miss, we need to get moving."

I scan the crowd to see if anyone can help. I'm not picky. But even though that might be the elf I'd seen earlier, over there up against the store, no one will meet my gaze. Cowards.

"Then take me too." Tears burn my eyes as I hold out my wrists for them to cuff. Let's face it, my life sucks pretty bad, and a warm bed and a free meal sound like just what Santa ordered.

The cop shakes his head, jots something down on a piece of paper, and hands it to me. "This is where we're taking him for questioning. You can come get him in a few hours unless someone presses charges."

The crowd dissipates as I stand there crying, my box of cookies my only comfort. The good news is that I still have seventeen cookies and the spare change from the burrito shop. Oh yeah, and a burrito that's stuffed in my coat pocket. The bad news is that my keys were in the bag the douchebag stole.

"June, can you give us a ride home?" Dina pulls her coat tight around her shoulders. "It's getting late, and I need to get Fred home." Fred's back at her side, his chin held high.

June sighs and looks at me. "Are you going to be okay?" She looks in her purse for keys.

I could tell her I have no way home, that everything I came with got stolen after she kicked me out of the caroling group. But I'm tired of leaning on everyone else to make my life easier. I mean, look where it's gotten me.

"I'm fine." I give her a half hug. "See you later."

We say our goodbyes, and I wander down the street,

one hand shoved in my pocket, the other clutching the cookies.

Can't a girl catch a break?

Chapter 10

There's this thing that happens when it snows. No matter how noisy a place is, the world seems to put its headphones on, muting everything. That's how it feels right now, as I trod aimlessly through the narrow swath of sidewalk visible through the snow.

The homeless guy from earlier is bundled inside a flimsy-looking sleeping bag, laying on cardboard in one of the doorways I pass. He's sporting a new red and white hat, with a matching scarf wrapped around his neck and gloves on his hands. "Hey, did you find Krampus?" he calls out.

I stop and look at him. "Yup. Found and lost him in the space of maybe ten minutes."

"Did you get what you needed?"

I feel so lost right now, so depleted that laying down in the snow sounds good. "Not exactly."

"What happened?"

"Not only did Krampus get arrested and is probably in jail right now." I cup a hand to my mouth and blow warm breath on it. "But my so-called friends left me here alone with no way home."

"People suck. Don't worry about Krampus. He'll find a way to make things right."

I make a scoffing noise. "Right. Krampus is going to save the day."

He smiles, sitting up. "You'll see. What's in that

box?" He nods to my security cookies.

"Apricot Kolaches. My oma's recipe. Want one?" I pop the box open.

He scootches over and pats an open space on the cardboard next to him. "Have a seat." He holds his hand out, accepting a cookie.

Soon we're both crunching on the buttery goodness, the apricots adding just the right amount of tartness to the sweet dough.

"This is the best cookie I've ever had." He wipes his mouth with the back of his hand.

"Thank you. You can have as many as you want."

We spend the next few minutes chomping on cookies, but his stomach is still growling.

"I have a burrito too, if you want it." I nod to the plastic bag dangling from my pocket.

His eyes brighten. "That would be delightful."

"I think it's frozen," I warn him, holding it out.

"Food is food." He tucks the wrapped burrito near his pillow of rolled-up clothes. "I'll save it for later."

Sitting here is much more tolerable than walking around, what with the warmth coming off him and the building blocking the cold wind and snow.

"Are you okay with me staying for a little bit?" I tuck my feet under me.

"Yeah, that's fine. It's warmer when it's more than one person."

I nod, nuzzling into the warmth of the stranger next to me. Good thing I can't smell anything anymore.

We watch as the street empties, folks from the contest packing up to go home. It looks like a snow globe out there, the light breeze lifting snow off the ground and spiraling it in the street.

We fall into a trance-like silence, broken only by the murmur of conversation from a random passerby or two. Maybe twenty minutes have passed when my bladder begins to scream. I knew I shouldn't have drunk that bottle of water June gave me. I struggle to stand, using the building to help me up.

The homeless guy starts awake. "Where you goin'?"

"Any tips on where to find a bathroom?"

Barely awake, he points down the street. It could be any number of businesses. Oh well.

"Thanks." I toss my last eleven cents into his cup before I go. My pockets are empty of everything but the business card the cop gave me. "Merry Christmas." I walk out onto the snow-covered sidewalk, hugging my cookies.

The mall across the street has restrooms, so I stomp my way through accumulated snow and wander around the mall's exterior. Ornaments overhead blink, and the light-wrapped Christmas trees add to the magic of the night.

I'm still thinking about the homeless guy, sleeping in the doorway across the street, perfectly content with what he has in life.

At least there are still some good people in the world.

****

I don't know what time it is, but the doors to the mall are locked. It's funny. I'm near where I was stuck in traffic, waiting for the cop to blow his whistle and let me turn the corner into the parking garage. I'd come here with so much to look forward to. Friends, singing, finally affirming my love for Harry. So anxious that something would go wrong. Did I bring this on myself?

I mean, look where I am now. The only thing I have left is a full bladder and a half-full plastic box of cookies. I move down the snow-covered street, stomping my feet to try and keep them from getting covered by snow.

I'm shivering so hard that my teeth are chattering by the time I cross the street and pass an alleyway, where a blip of red hair catches my eye. I take three more steps before it hits me to stop. When I turn around and kick through the snow to walk into the dimly lit corridor, I call out, "Fred? Is that you?"

Something is moving around inside the dumpster. It kinda sounds like a human-sized rat looking for food. Thankfully, there are only drifts of snow here and there, the fire escape platforms and ladders on both buildings blocking the dumpster and alleyway below.

"It's in here somewhere," a muffled voice says.

I climb up the bin and peek over the side. Fred is crouched inside, sorting through the garbage.

"Why are you in a dumpster?" I hop down and lean against the stinky metal container.

"Because I lost my lighter when I was at the cookie booth."

I have to laugh. "Are you sure it's here? Couldn't it have been buried by the snow?"

"Nah, saw the guy pick it up and toss it in the bin."

"You couldn't need it that bad," I say.

"You couldn't need it that bad," he says in a falsetto voice, mocking me as more things move around, banging the walls of the container.

"Where's your mom?"

Fred peeks over the side. He's even dirtier than the last time I saw him. "I don't know. Home probably. She screamed at me all the way back to the car and then told me I could find my own way home."

I stomp my feet to try and get feeling back into them. "And why are you looking for your lighter?" It's weird, but I'm kind of getting used to the cold.

"To keep me warm, duh." He dives into another section of the bin.

"Well, did you learn your lesson?" I mean, maybe he doesn't need to go to hell. Maybe it's a good thing Krampus is in jail, and Fred will grow out of this ass-holery he's up to right now.

"Found it," he says from inside of the bin.

Great. Just what the world needs, more Fires by Fred™.

"What do you mean, *lesson*?" he asks, surprising me by hopping over the side and landing at my side. He flicks the lighter, trying to get a flame. That sound makes me twitch.

"Like, you know you were naughty, right? You know that throwing things at people's heads and setting skirts and tents on fire are all bad, right?"

"I was just having fun," he says. "You're over-reacting." He reaches out and wrestles the cookies from me. "Can I have one now?" he shoves one inside his mouth and grabs another.

Then again, maybe some people never change. I widen my eyes at him and grab the box back. "I didn't say yes."

He smiles and chews with his mouth open, crumbs spraying out. "Good cookies."

In the hushed evening air, a soft *clip-clop* sound gets closer to us. Seattle uses equine police during events, and I did see a few out and about in the distance tonight. Wait a minute. Maybe they're here to arrest me too. Now, that could work out. My bladder spasms; not a good sign. They'll let me use the restroom at the station, no doubt.

The lighter ignites, and I watch in astonishment as Fred picks up a piece of trash off the ground, catches it on fire, then throws it into the dumpster. "What the hell are you doing?"

"We need heat." He steps back.

We stand there, next to each other, waiting. After a minute, I'm convinced it must have burnt out. When I climb up and peer over the edge of the bin, I can't even see the charred piece of garbage, let alone tendrils of smoke or the beginning of flames.

Fred climbs up too. "Huh." He scratches his head and flings one leg over, crawling back in with a hollow thud.

"Stop!" I drop back onto the ground and crouch to try and hold some heat in, rubbing my hands together. "That's not safe." But honestly? I'm past caring what he does.

A muffled answer doesn't quite make it to my ears. He crawls out, hangs over the edge of the bin, and shakes something green.

My mouth is dry, and the ends of my fingers ache and burn. I'm so cold my body no longer tingles. Numbness is the name of the game, thankfully dulling the pain of my full bladder. My eyes are closed, and I'm beginning to nod off to that *clip-clop* sound growing closer.

A loud bang fills the night, waking me up in time to see the lid of the dumpster bang closed, then fly open. My bladder lets go, the warmth from the pee welcome against the cold ground.

Fred has a look of awe on his face.

"What did you do?" My heart is thudding so hard it feels like it's trying to claw out of my chest. I cover my head against the flames shooting out.

"There was an almost empty green gas thing that people use for cooking when they're camping," he says. My ears ring from the blast, so the words are muffled. "I used this to depress the valve and then lit the fumes." He holds up a knife that's silhouetted by raging flames.

I adjust myself, ashamed of my lack of bladder control. Sadly, the urine has cooled, and now my crotch just feels icky. "That's thinking." My cheeks feel violated by the heat, my eyes by the bright light.

He starts sniffing, "Why does it smell like piss?"

My chest tingles in embarrassment. "We're in an alleyway dumb-ass, what do you expect?" The feeling is returning to my fingers, though my toes are still frozen solid.

The *clip-clop* is faster and closer now. Fred is alert, looking around for the sound. We can't see anything, just the snow swirling in the air and the bright fire before us. And then, like an angel stepping out of the snow, there's Krampus, *real* Krampus, heading into the alley at a clip.

Chapter 11

Krampus growls, his eyes locked on Fred. The drifts of snow have grown higher, glistening in the firelight.

"You came back," I say. Krampus looks at me, his eyes softening. The moment of joy that comes to his face sends a rush through my body.

The homeless guy was right. Krampus didn't leave me here alone, after all.

Krampus bows, his lips curving. "Of course, my lady."

"How did you get free?"

He gives me this sexy half-smile. "A little bit of magic."

A wave of happiness washes through me. I guess it's time for me to believe in Santa.

Fred inches away. I reach out and grab the little shit by the ear, pulling him to stand at my side.

The kid yelps in shock. "Let go!"

"Nope." This entire night is making me contemplate life like I never have before.

Fred is a shit, all the way down to his soul. He'll grow up to be a bad man with no empathy who burns down buildings for fun. That is to say, if he doesn't get worse.

"You know, we never talked about what you do with the kids once you catch them," I say to Krampus. I size him up from head to hoof. This beautiful barrel-chested man is clearly a real creature standing in front of me, not a loser dressed in a costume. How had I ever thought otherwise?

"If cooperation is evident, I place them in the bag, and they slide through a magical tube straight to the underworld."

"There's a door in there?" I point to his wicker basket. Well, if monsters are real, then I guess doors in bags can be real too.

He takes the wicker satchel off of his back and lets me look inside. "Not a door. It is…" He looks off to the left as if to find the perfect word. "It is more magical than that."

"I can't see anything." I move the birch branches out of the way to see the bottom of the bag. "Just looks like it goes on forever."

"This is a bag of holding."

"Like that girl's bag in the book about wizards?" I ponder what this means. If Krampus is real, are magic schools real too?

"I do not know this wizard person. But Santa told me it is similar to the bags of holding humans use when they play role-playing games."

"Huh." Fred tries to crane around to look inside the bag. He's got more black smudges on his face, obscuring the smeared chocolate.

If this is real, what other things in folklore were telling us the truth, warning us of possible pitfalls in life?

"Is the Easter Bunny real too?"

Krampus's brows go together again. "I know of the name, but I do not think so. It is just Santa, the Tooth Fairy, and me at the dinner table during family reunions. And their mates."

It had never occurred to me that he might have someone waiting for him back—wherever he lives. I mean, Santa said he was lonely, but maybe he doesn't know everything.

"Is Mrs. Krampus back at home waiting for you?"

"No, I do not have a mate," he says.

Fred is trying to get away, but I stomp on his foot.

"Ouch," he says. "You're abusing me."

"And where is home?" I ask.

"Antarctica."

A shiver runs through me, but it occurs to me that this is why he's all covered in fur and why he doesn't seem phased by the extreme temperatures. "I see."

"I apologize, my lady. I wish to talk to you for the rest of time, but first, I must attend to the Naughty List."

I nod, beginning to accept the fact that I'm massively crushing on a man that sends children to hell.

"Okay then, let's do this." I turn to Fred. "I think it's time for you to go."

Krampus walks toward us. The kid's shoulders tense, his body goes rigid.

Krampus reaches out for Fred, but I stop him, remembering something he said earlier.

"He'll just go *woosh* and go to…?"

Krampus nods. "*Woosh.* Straight to hell."

Fred is paler than I've ever seen him, the dark smudges standing out. I almost feel bad for him. "Can't say I won't be joining you when the time comes, but it's time for you to go." I turn to Krampus. "Hold the child's legs together, please?"

"May I have a cookie first?" Krampus's beautiful wide eyes are dilated in desire.

"Of course." I hand him the box.

And that, boys and girls, is how Opa Krampus knew that Miss Khalie was the woman of his dreams.

Werewolves Prefer Shortbread

by

Dakota Issacs

Christmas Cookies Series

Dedication

For my Mom and Dad, who shouldn't be surprised I write love stories, because I grew up watching theirs.

Chapter One

Callum

I have a list of more things than I could possibly accomplish today. All of them require my immediate attention, yet I find myself standing outside a bakery window mesmerized by the shortbread cookies on display. It sounds cliché even to me, but they remind me of home. And these cookies don't look like pale American imitations. They are stamped in the traditional manner and have a nice golden edge, and I can see the butter glisten. Someone with business sense has propped the front door open. The smell is a powerful lure: a perfect blend of cinnamon, smoke, and fresh vanilla. Sweet but not cloying.

This is no time for indulgence, but I find myself walking through the door anyway. It's probably too quiet a town to have a decent espresso, but a cup of coffee will do me good, and I can bring some treats home for the girls. They are in desperate need of spoiling.

The line for the counter snakes all the way back to the door, but I can't leave now. I've spotted cupcakes all done up in pastel buttercream and topped with tiny unicorn heads complete with silver horns. I know the girls will love them. Especially Maise who's been stuck inside the house for weeks now.

Someone has a good eye. The shop is understated

and warm with exposed brick and pressed tin ceilings. The walls are hung with cheeky oil paintings of people of all ages biting into cupcakes with blissful expressions on their faces. The artist's palette echoes the same pastel hues as the baked goods. The requisite Christmas tree is decorated with tiny ornaments depicting an array of baked goods and trimmed with twinkling fairy lights. Put one of these shops in Glasgow and they'd probably have a line out the door as well. I wonder if the owner has thought of turning this into a franchise. If the baked goods are as good as the décor, I may approach them about investing. I scan the room for the name of the bakery and find a pink neon sign hanging behind the counter. *Crave Bakery*. I like the name.

I catch a glimpse of denim-colored curls and my heart tugs strangely in my chest. When the woman stands up, my suspicions are confirmed. I'm staring into the face of Lily Harris, the woman who hates me. She gives me a glare that says she's recognized me as well. I think about turning to leave, but I haven't done anything wrong. I didn't know she worked here. And any opportunity to give the girls a little joy is one I'm going to take. I put a neutral expression on my face and start to scroll through the messages on my phone. I can answer a few emails while I wait. I try to focus on the words in front of me, yet I can't help sneaking glances at her. Even with the troubled look on her face she's lovely. She's a tiny thing but even in a pair of overalls you can catch a glimpse of her curves. She's a fearless looking lass with her wild blue curls, and exquisite sleeves of floral tattoos on her forearms. She looks joyfully alive, free. Like a woman I'd want to get to know. If she didn't hate me. And if I had the luxury of dating anyone right now.

Which I don't.

Besides, I don't know her, not really. I've only met her once. Her last words to me were "You are doing a cruel thing. Shame on you." I've replayed the conversation several times. I did what had to be done. And I must live with it. I suspect she's not the only person in town who dislikes me. I can't worry about that. I have responsibilities now. Three of them. I can't spare thoughts about a woman I barely know. Even if she wakes my wolf. I've turned the problem of her hatred over and over in mind, trying to think of ways to explain myself. I can't think of any lies that would make her like me and I certainly can't tell her the truth. Even if my wolf cried out *mine* the first time she walked into my sitting room. It's not her. It's more likely that my wolf sees her as a walking representation of freedom. The one thing we are both being denied.

Chapter Two

Lily

I cannot believe Callum McAllister has the nerve to walk into my bakery. Last Wednesday he evicted my Grandma from the home she's lived in for over forty years. The man inherited a twenty-two-room mansion and he's worried about a three-bedroom cottage that sits on the edge of his property.

I was sure that I could talk him out of it. That once he saw a human face, he could be convinced to change his mind. He wouldn't even let me argue my case. "I'm sorry for your trouble but we will not be renewing the lease." And then he stood up and left the room. Who does that? Who just walks out of a conversation? But that's what Callum McAllister did, sending his sheepish looking personal assistant into the room to escort me out.

I itch to throw him out on his ass. Half the people in this shop would probably applaud, but my good sense takes over. I don't want drama in my shop. It's not good for business. A bakery should be a warm and welcoming place. All the time. Still if that idiot thinks I'm going to wait on him he's got another thing coming. We're in the middle of our afternoon rush so I try to push the distracting thoughts out of my mind and fix a smile onto my face as I fill people's orders.

"My sister-in-law raves about this place. What's the

best thing on the menu?"

The young woman in the cute pink sweater is asking the wrong question. So, I ask the right one. "Depends. What was your favorite treat as a kid?"

"Peanut butter and chocolate chip cookies." She doesn't even have to think about it. My kind of girl.

"Easy. You want a Nutty Tuxedo Cupcake. Dark chocolate cupcake stuffed with a rich peanut butter cream cheese surprise in the center."

"Sold. I'll have one of those, a coffee light and sweet and could I get a dozen assorted cookies to go. I'm bringing a treat back to the office."

"If you have a business card, drop it in the jar. Each week we do an office giveaway. You could win coffee and pastries for your whole office."

"Awesome." Yeah, its awesome, the weekly promotion has helped me build up a solid mailing list with a minimal outlay of expense. I've learned most people will open a promotional email with free cookies in the subject line. And once I've got people in the door they always come back for more. A quality bake good is everyone's friend.

I fill her order and work my way through the line. I wait until he's standing in front of me. He starts to place his order, all business. I take a deep breath, look him in the eye, and walk away.

"Take over the counter," I whisper to Janie, my barista. Then I push through the double doors and walk into the kitchen.

Chapter Three

Callum

"I can't believe she just walked away from you like that." My sister-in-law fights a smile. But she must see the look on my face because the smile quickly becomes a look of concern.

"Okay. You want the truth? Walking out of the room like that when she came over to see you? Dumb move. I know you don't like to waste time, but you should have let her say her piece. The rest of it? Not your fault. You did the hard thing. It had to be done. The girls need to be protected. And I'm sorry you're the one who looks like the villain of the story."

"I knew it was a mistake as soon as I walked out the door. But I didn't think she was a waste of time, Fi. It wasn't like that. I just didn't know what else to say. Truth is I felt like shite about it. We threw her Grandma out of a house she's called home for decades. Nothing I can say makes that right. The lass was right to walk away from me. I just hope she doesn't get in trouble with her boss over it."

"Don't think we have to worry about her getting in trouble with the boss." My brother wanders into the kitchen and gives me an accusing look. "Were you gonna tell me there were sweets?" He reaches for a cookie and his wife swats his hand away.

"We are waiting for the girls to wake up from their naps. Then you'll get your tea."

Brodie pulls his wife out of her chair, and takes the seat, gently pulling her back onto his lap. He has that dazed look of adoration on his face that he wears every time he's in the same room with her. Sickening. And a part of me longs to feel the same way. I try to push those ridiculous thoughts out of my brain and focus on the conversation.

"You're looking a little out of it big brother. Are you paying attention? The woman can't get in trouble with the boss. She is the boss, you eejit. She's some sort of baking wunderkind. When she was seventeen her Grandad gave her a loan and helped her buy a food truck. Vinnie's pizzeria let her sell cookies in their parking lot. She was a runaway success and took her profits and opened that bakery when she was only twenty. Took some sort of Culinary Arts program at a nearby community college. Big local success story."

That bakery is no small achievement. The espresso was spot on and so was the pistachio short bread. The barista tried to sell me on the white chocolate grapefruit, but I told her those weren't for me.

"I'll stick with the classics thank you. To a Scot those other flavors are an abomination."

"Your loss, the baker here is a genius," she'd said with a smile.

"How'd you find all this out?"

"It's called Google; you've never heard of it?"

"Funny."

"Actually, I visited the local barbershop. Started a conversation. The locals don't seem so happy that we moved Grandma out. I'd say the general tone was cool and polite. But we didn't have a choice. You need to remember that, brother. The girls need a place to safely roam. And until they learn to control their shift, we need to protect them. Plus, I heard the old lady used to warn off coyotes with a shotgun full of buckshot. Can you imagine if she'd seen a wolf? What if she shot at one of the girls? The locals will come around eventually. Even Lily."

I don't answer because the girls are up from their naps and making their way shyly into the kitchen. I wonder how long it's going to take for them to feel at home here. I remember what it was like growing up in our house. My mum had to shout 'walk don't run' several times a day. My siblings were wild, noisy, joyful creatures. These girls have a wary quiet about them that kills me. At least they don't smell of fear anymore, that was heartbreaking.

"Finally, sleepy heads," my brother says, "I thought I was going to have to eat all the cupcakes myself."

That earns him a smile.

"There are cupcakes?" Rowen asks.

"Aye, and these are not your average cupcakes. Callum's brought you magic Unicorn cupcakes." Brodie turns the box toward them.

This earns some squeals that make them sound more like average six-year-old girls. It's a wonderful sound, and I wrap my arms around them and give them a hug.

"I'll pour the tea." Fiona gets up to tend to the kettle.

****

The cupcakes are a huge success. Maisie insists her unicorn is too pretty to eat and must be saved. I'm not sure how long a creature made from sugar will last. But I think I can find some unicorn stuffies to take their place.

Brodie gives his wife a look.

"Come on girls. Let's run off that sugar." They head off to the tack room to change out of their clothes. I feel the rippling power of their shift and then they are out in the yard heading for the woods. A beautiful silver wolf, and three steel grey pups.

I'm sure Fiona planned the run so Brodie could do a mental health checkup on his big brother.

"The girls are going to be fine. It will just take some time to adjust."

"You're assuming a lot because we've never seen anything like this before."

My Da is head of the most powerful were clan in Scotland. Our history has been carefully preserved and it was taught to us from the time we learned to speak. There are two ways to become a lupine. You are born into it. Or you are bitten. Although that practice has been forbidden in Scotland for the last fifty years.

A month ago, there were reports of strange happenings at a group home on the outskirts of Glasgow. A problem with wolves. They'd managed to get inside the facility and tear apart the kitchens. Made it onto the security cameras and the nightly news. Local gossip was a trio of girls were turning into wolves as they slept.

Outlandish, but Mam was sent to investigate. She said she could feel them before she'd even made it through the door. She pulled every string she could and made some generous contributions. Now the girls are in our care. It was safer to pull them out of the Country for a while. Let the gossip wind down. Give them time to adjust to the change. The change which as far as we know has never happened to anyone before they hit puberty. The girls are the youngest shifters we've ever seen. Three six-year-old girls completely unrelated to each other, with no shifter blood in their family lines that we can ascertain. And Ma and Fiona have broached the subject many times in the gentlest way, but it seems like the girls were never bitten. If they were not a single mark remains. They are a complete mystery. My Da has been handing down his responsibilities these past few years so it seemed wrong to have my parents move to a strange country and raise a family all over again. I volunteered. Fi and my brother offered to come as well. But they have a baby on the way, and I know Fi wants to have that baby on Scottish soil. I can't rely on them to be a permanent solution. And as hard as it is to explain, when my Wolf saw those girls, he shouted *Mine.* We had secluded property in the States. It made sense at the time. Now they are in my care and I feel overwhelmed nearly every minute of every day. I don't know why I thought I could do this. I know nothing about six-year-old girls. I certainly didn't think I could feel this overpowering love for them. Not like this. Not so soon. But I do. I love them as surely as they were mine, and I will do whatever it takes for them to feel loved and secure. Safe. I need the community to embrace us and I'm not sure how to do that. Make them care about some rich outsiders who cast a beloved local out of her home. When the girls can all control their shift, they'll need to be in school. I want them to be accepted.

My brother seems to sense everything I'm thinking. "Just do your best, Callum."

"What if it's not enough."

"Love is always enough."

Chapter Four

Lily

"You've got to learn to tell better stories."

"What?" I have no idea what Janie is talking about. It's four o'clock and our day is almost done. The front door is locked, and we've been turning over the chairs so the porter can mop in a peaceable silence.

"You tell me all about this ass-hole who evicted your Grandma, and you never said he was gorgeous."

"He's not…"

"Listen I know he's our sworn enemy. I promise to never date him, but you have to admit he is hands down the most handsome man who's ever walked through this door. Lily, he's hot."

"He just doesn't do it for it me."

Okay, that's such a lie. The man is so good looking the first time I saw him he literally took my breath away. He's got to be at least six three and all of it is muscle. And I've always thought long hair on a guy was not my thing. Wrong. I was oh so wrong. His hair falls just past his shoulders in an inky black sheet. It's so glossy you want to reach out and touch it. In fact, all of him looks insanely touchable. Insane being the operative word. Because he is not a nice guy.

"He has crap taste in food though. He said your white chocolate grapefruit shortbread sounded like an abomination."

"He did not. They are a perfectly balanced cookie, not too tart, not too sweet. I can't believe he had the nerve to insult my food."

Janie starts to laugh. "The look on your face. If I were Callum McAllister, I would go into hiding."

****

After work I give Gram a call.

"Sweetheart it's so good to hear your voice. Did you get the pictures I sent you? I cannot wait for you to see the apartment. It's so decadent. It even has a spa tub in the bathroom. There's a coffee shop called the Lazy Llama just a block away. It's the cutest thing you've ever seen. Tiny. Their scones have nothing on yours, but I took a chair by the window and just people watched this morning. It's just so alive here. I got you an adorable bracelet at this little boutique on 3rd Street. I thought I would get more turned around on these streets. But I've only gotten lost once. Turned the Google maps you put on my phone on, and I was fine. Jill and Wendy are picking me up in a little while. We're going to see a show at the New York Theater Workshop. It's gotten a lot of buzz. They say it's going to get picked up for Broadway. Then we are going for a late dinner at this Turkish restaurant they love. How are things with you, sweetheart?"

She sounds elated. So, I don't say any of the things I want to.

"I'm great. Trying out a new line of shortbread cookies. Gonna push the envelope a little and see what happens. Got a couple new standing office orders, so that's great."

"Do you have any plans for tonight?"

"Yeah," I lie. "Janie and I are going to go to Lennie's for some burgers." *Wonderful. Lying to my Gram. Who am I?*

"Have fun, honey, and try not to work too hard."

I ask her some questions about her adventures and try to sound excited. Then I get off the phone and throw a frozen pizza into the oven.

I shouldn't be this angry. I know it wasn't our house. And I know I didn't live there anymore. I've been out of that house for a year now, but I'm still so full of rage that I want to hit something. I feel like if I lose that house then I'll lose the memories. Stupid right? But it's how I feel whether it makes sense or not. I lose things. And I am so freaking tired of it. I lost my Mom and Dad when I was four to a triple car pile-up. Grandpa who was like a father, died last year. And now that Grandma is not tethered to that house, I feel like she's going to drift away too. And then I hate myself for feeling that way. It's shitty and it's petty because she's raised two families and lost her husband. If she wants to live in Manhattan and take some happiness for herself then who am I to stand in her way. But I feel so alone. It's not like he loves that house. He's not going to live in it. We've lost it because he is self-centered and super rich and *values his privacy.* The timer for the pizza dings and I realize I don't feel like eating. Might as well head back to the kitchen where I take my frustrations out on some dough. Mr. McMansion thinks a grapefruit-white chocolate shortbread is an abomination? He has no idea.

Chapter Five

Callum

In one way the house is perfect. Isolated and remote, it sits on twenty-three acres of untouched forest land. For protecting three untrained shifters it's great. But for raising children. Awful. It's too damn big, and too well appointed. If I were a kid, I would be constantly worried I'd break things. It's too sterile and eerily quiet. It doesn't even have a swing set. That at least I can fix. There's a home goods store a mile out of town. They opened at 6 am, so I've already loaded the car with everything I'll need. A swing set with two slides, and a little wooden cottage with its own dainty door and two windows. The girls can help paint and decorate it. We'll even add some twinkling lights. I turn off the highway and onto the little two-lane road that takes me home. Right past the bakery that houses tastes of home, and the lovely lass who hates me. Even though I shouldn't I turn into the parking lot.

She's changed her window display. The shelves and the wire baskets are gone. Instead, the edges of the glass are frosted with snowflakes. An elegantly lettered sign sits on a wooden easel. *The Abominable Snowmen Shortbreads have arrived.* And on the opposite easel: *For the sophisticated cookie lover: Introducing our artisanal shortbreads: Chai latte, Peanut butter Miso and Nutella Hot Cocoa.* I can't help it. I start to laugh, getting some strange looks from the people passing by to get in line. The barista must have passed on my comments. Never expected to get such a reaction. The woman is talented as hell. Dozens of abominable snowmen, with googly eyes, and coconut fur are enjoying their holiday season. Some are decorating a paper tree. Others are wrapping gifts. Some are roasting marshmallows over paper flames. How did she find cookie cutters in a variety of poses? Did she cut them out freehand? I would think this display took days to create. But I'm sure my comments yesterday incited this work of art. How did she do this in a day? Oh Lord, the hairiest one is on ladder putting a star atop the tree. It has massive brows and a crazy look on its face. It's also wearing a kilt in McAllister plaid and knee-high plaid stockings. I pull out my phone and start to take some pictures for the girls.

"Can't get enough of my abominations. Need to memorialize them on film?"

I love her voice, even when she's berating me. It's got this little scratch to it. It's sexy as hell. I could listen to her for hours.

"The window is magnificent. I've got three little girls at home who think you've hung the moon. I know they'll want to see this."

She looks speechless. First time I've seen that look on her face. She also looks exhausted.

"Are you feeling all right, Lass?"

"I'm fine. Why are you here?"

"I came to apologize." She really doesn't look good. And I think I know the reason why.

"Did you work through the night?" I am familiar with workaholics. Being that I'm one myself.

She just gives me a scowl.

"Lily, answer me. Did you work all night long?"

"Is yelling at people your idea of an apology? Is that how they do things in Scotland?"

"You know what, you don't even have to answer the question because I'm familiar with the look. You baked through the night, didn't you?"

"That would be none of your business, but I'm fine. I'm actually on my way home."

"You're not planning to drive, are you?"

Chapter Six

Lily

Now that he's said it, I realize it's a stupid idea. Driving home on no sleep.

"You're actually right. Don't get used to it. I'll call an Uber."

What is he doing back at my shop? Still, it sends a little thrill down my spine. I wonder if he saw the cookie snowman in the kilt. It's the McAllister plaid. I know. I Googled it. And I hope he noticed my artisanal flavors. He was taking pictures. Does that mean he likes my work? My heart skips in my chest. I Don't know why. Probably just the sleep deprivation. Oh, and the little fact that Callum in a worn hoodie and jeans is even better looking than Callum in a suit. How is that even possible? Why are the worst guys always the hottest? So wrong.

"Lily. Lily, are you all right? You look like you're ready to fall over. Please let me drive you home."

I shouldn't. No rides with the enemy. But I am so tired.

"Okay. But hold on just one moment. Let me tell Janie. You know in case I disappear or anything."

I expect a smart-ass remark in return. But all he says is "That's a good idea."

I actually want to go in and grab some cookies for the kids. Which according to local gossip are not his, but the orphaned children of close family friends that he has taken responsibility for. Which is odd because he's a thirty-something supposedly single guy and it's also lovely. That he would step in where he's needed. Well, lovely and weird.

I head back in and fill one box with snowmen. Including a couple in kilts. Then I fill another box with a mix of my artisanal shortbreads.

When I come back out, he glances down at the boxes wrapped in pink and orange ribbon, but he doesn't say a word. Instead, he opens my door.

"Have you eaten?"

I think I've fallen off the sanity ledge, but I'm also starving. I've eaten a few deformed snowmen but nothing you'd call real food.

"No. I skipped dinner last night."

He makes a sound of disapproval but doesn't use his words.

Instead, he pulls into the parking lot of Eddie's Diner.

"Running your body into the ground is not good business sense. "

And then he's opening my car door, and we're walking inside.

"You don't talk much," I say to him. That's not really a criticism. There's something calming about the silence.

"I owe you so many apologies I was trying to figure out where to start."

Okay.

He stands at the register, too polite to seat himself. But that's how we do things around here.

"Follow me." I lead him back to the corner booth.

No matter where I put him, he's going to be the center of attention. He's the new person in town. Haven't had one of those in a year. He's also insanely hot so there is that.

Maggie approaches as soon as we sit.

"Coffee?" she asks. I chose her section because she's the fastest waitress here. Queen of the turn and burn. I would have poached her for the bakery but it's not good form. Also, I didn't want to get myself banned from the only diner in town.

"Yes please." Callum answers yes as well.

"Need a menu?" she asks him.

"Do you know what you'd like, Lily?" he asks.

"Eggs over easy, turkey bacon, home fries, burn them please, and sourdough toast. Oh, and could I have an order of the triple berry pancakes."

He doesn't even raise a brow at the impressive over order. "I'll have the same please. Thank you."

Maggie leaves to pour the coffees. And I study my fingertips, so I won't be tempted to stare at Callum.

"Let's start with your food, shall we. You're baking is impeccable, but I think you know that. Obviously, I'm an eegit because your pistachio shortbreads were heavenly, and I have a feeling that white chocolate grapefruit cookie that I mocked is nothing short of perfection. In fact, when you caught me eyeing your window, I was on my way to try one. So, I owe you an apology."

"All right."

Inside my five-year-old is jumping up and down. *He likes my food. He thinks it's impeccable.* I love that word. I am so glad that I tossed some grapefruit cookies into the box. But I try to keep my poker face on. He doesn't need to know my heart is doing cartwheels at his praise.

Maggie comes back with our coffees, and a big pitcher of maple syrup.

We thank her and Callum waits till she's walked away before he continues.

"The other apology is harder. Because I am sorry. More than you know. I should have listened to what you had to say. It wasn't well done of me to dismiss you like that. And I'm sorry you and your Grandma are hurting. I truly am. But I would make the same decision again. I need to do what's best for the girls. They are having a rough time of it and they need their privacy right now."

Okay. That makes no sense. Oh, what the hell, no need to censor conversation with a man I'm never going to see again.

"All right. Since we are having a polite conversation, I'm going to give this a try. About my food. You're totally forgiven. But about the house. I just don't get it. My Grandma's not a threat to three little girls. Are you afraid she'd want to babysit? Pepper you with unsolicited parenting advice? Ply them with chocolate chip cookies. I'm not sure what the polite word is, but you sound a little crazy. And take it from someone who knows: isolating someone who's grieving is not the best idea."

"I don't expect you to understand," he says softly. "Nor to accept my apology. I just wanted you to know I am sorry for hurting you. The truth is I don't know how to do any of this. Not really. I'm just trying to keep my head above water right now."

He just had to say that. Now it's impossible to hate him. Even if he does sound overprotective and crazy. And even if he made the wrong choice. What the hell? Sometimes you have to be the bigger person.

"It's all right, Callum. We're all right. I think you made the wrong choice. But it's your house and your choice to make. This must all be overwhelming."

Chapter Seven

Callum

"It's all right. We're all right."

Out of all the things I thought she might say, I never thought she'd say that. Because it can't be all right. Not really. I couldn't even explain. Not properly. And just like that she's willing to forgive me? Who is this woman?

The food arrives. Big platters that nearly take up the whole table. Lily digs in with gusto. I just stare at her in awe.

"How can we be okay?"

She looks at me with a wry arch of her brow. "Trying to get me to change my mind? Gotta say you're a weird one."

She has no idea. But she just gives me a small smile and picks up her fork.

"I do understand that life can be hard. And my Gram does adore her loaner apartment so there is that. She reminded me that life is change. If she doesn't hold a grudge, why should I? Are the girls all really six years old?"

"Yes, Maisie, Rowen and Kasey."

"Six is fun. Did they find the secret bookshelf in the library yet? That was always my favorite."

Of course, wolves would have secret passages.

"I'm not sure I want them to know. What if they get stuck?"

"There are doors that lead out as well. If you're really worried, I guess you could seal them up. Or you could just put some lights in the passageways. That's what I'd do."

"Could you show me?"

I have no right to ask.

"Yeah."

"It doesn't have to be now. You need your sleep."

"No, now works. Might as well get it over with. You can drop me off after. I'm not that far away."

Of course, she'd want to minimize her contact with me. Nobody likes to hang out with overprotective weirdos. But it still hurts to get dismissed like that. Like I'm a trip to the dentist for a bad molar.

"May I ask you a question?" I'm not ready to give up her company. Not just yet.

She gives me another arch of her eyebrow. "That would depend on the question?"

"How did you get that display up in a night?"

She grins.

"Cheated. I'd already bought the cardboard cutouts of the tree, and the packages. I had these mini polar bear stuffed animals. I was going to put them in the window, wearing these little orange and fuchsia scarves. You know, the shop colors. Then you called my shortbreads abominations, and I had a better idea. Abominable shortbread snowman. Thanks for that by the way. They are going to be sold out in no time."

"I have no doubt. Did you take many business classes?"

"Just a couple that were required. The first thing I

did when I opened the shop was hire a bookkeeper I trust. But I still go over the books every week."

"Smart."

I ask her more questions about her shop. She's a natural. Put her in charge of a corporation and I have no doubt she could lead them to a spot in the Fortune 500. But my favorite part of all this business talk is the way her face lights up when she speaks about it. It takes her from beautiful to heartbreaking perfection. I'll be dreaming of that look on her face. My wolf has calmed considerably. He thinks we are going to keep her. If only I could.

"What about you?" she asks. "All this business talk. What do you run? It's not a small nation, is it? I'm afraid to ask?"

"No. Honestly, it started with comic books."

She grins. "I love comic books."

I tell her about my love of comics and how I started to buy and sell them. They proved to be a popular obsession, and I like to think I have a keen eye for splendid things. I managed to buy a store and turned that into four. When I felt they could run themselves without a lot of supervision I turned my obsessive mind to great Italian food which I felt we had an utter lack of in Scotland. I started with one restaurant and now I have seven.

By the time I finish telling my story, we've lingered over coffee for an hour. The second time I ask for more coffee, the waitress gives me a death glare and the bill, with a terse "you pay upfront." I get that time is money, and the more customers she waits on, the more money she'll acquire. Simple. So, I tip her well. Like down payment on a house well. After that, the coffee flows free, and she even attempts a smile.

"We should probably go. You have secret passages to seal up, and a swing set to build."

"That I do." I want to take this moment and spin it out. Linger in it. If this were any other time in my life, I wouldn't let this woman go. I stand up and offer her my hand to help her out of the booth.

Chapter Eight

Lily

"You all right, Lass? He chuckles. I look up to see him grinning at me. We are standing at the cash register and he's trying to pay the bill. But he needs both hands to open his wallet and take out his card. And I'm still holding one. I let it drop and step away. It just felt so good. Warm. Right. I wasn't thinking. Is this sleep deprived psychosis?

Maybe I should just take you home?" he says.

"No. With kids in the house, you want to be safe. You should know where the passages are at least. It will just take a few minutes."

"If you're sure you're all right?"

Now the cashier is staring at me too.

"I just need sleep. That's all. Easy problem to fix." I give them both a quick smile, and hope my face isn't the color of a tomato.

I'm not fine. Breakfast with a strange man is the erotic highlight of my dating life. Just holding his hand. I felt that touch everywhere. It can't be normal. I want to hold his hand again. Right now. I want to lean up on my toes, grab a fistful of his hair, pull him toward me and kiss him until I can't remember my name. And that's just the start of what I'd like to do with him. I really need to get out more. Try to work on my nonexistent social life.

Stop putting everything into my career. My reaction to him is simply because he's there. My body senses a male body nearby and it reacts. That's all. Of course, it helps that he's a male body whose eyes didn't glaze over when I started to talk business. It seemed like I could talk to him for hours and he'd listen. More than that, he'd understand. And at first, I thought rich guy. He'll just be stuffy. Now I'm starting to think he's a little bit shy around strangers, but with a wry sense of humor you might miss if you weren't paying close attention. And the accent. It does strange things to me. I start to imagine the things he might say if we were alone together. Everything sounds better with a brogue. That's it. He's just exotic. A novelty. We don't get a lot of new things in this town. His appeal will wear off. It's got to. Because even though I don't want to carry around anger at him, it's hard to see myself with the man who evicted my Gram.

****

The house looks better. More like a home. Someone's taken the velvet tufted settees, and the hard wooden chairs with no cushions that looked like they belonged in a museum and replaced them with oversized sofas and afghans that shout comfortable. A couple teddy bears, and a stuffed goat are piled in a corner. Picture books are scattered on the coffee table.

I can hear voices coming from the kitchen. I'm not sure if he wants me to meet his family. He's weirdly private. "Let me show you the trigger for the door in the library first" I say, so he won't feel like I expect him to introduce me, "and then I can show you where it leads. There is a secret stairway in the wall that takes you all the way to the attic."

"Is this the Goddess of baked good?" The man walking into the living room must be his brother. He's also ridiculously tall, with the same blue-green eyes. Although this brother smiles.

"Hi, I'm Brodie, the younger brother." Three girls come to stand beside him looking shy. "This is Maisie, Kasey and Rowen." He says with a hand atop each head. "And this is Miss Harris: the maker of those cupcakes you loved so much."

"Lily's fine." I say to him. "If that's all right with you."

"Lily it is. My wife is shopping. We are working on the girl's rooms. But she'll be sorry she missed you. She was impressed by your baking."

Maisie—at least I'm fairly sure it's Maisie—comes over and thrusts a piece of paper in my hands.

"This is for me? Thank you."

A brightly colored unicorn is flying, as three girls on the ground wave to him. It's surprisingly good. Chagall like. She's shaded the unicorn. And drawn the features of the people. Not just dots for the eyes, and a half circle for the mouth.

"This is beautiful. Thank you."

"I kept her."

"She means the Unicorn." Callum says. "Thought it was too beautiful to eat. The rest of us weren't as highly principled."

"They are not too hard to make. I have cupcake making classes every Saturday. You could make a unicorn, or a koala bear or a cat, and you don't have to eat it unless you want to."

"Maisie's not allowed out yet. Not til she's better." Rowen says. *She lost her Mom and Dad and she's sick?*

"Well, I hope you feel better soon, and when you do I hope you'll stop by."

"Or you could come here. We have a kitchen." Rowen says.

Helpful girl.

"It's really hard for Maisie to be stuck in the house all day. She's only six, and she loved your cupcakes. Please come here. Please."

Her angelic features are schooled into an earnest expression. But I feel like I'm getting played by a top-level negotiator. She knows there is no nice way for me to say no.

"I'd be happy to come over. If it's all right with Callum."

There. Let him be the one to tell them no.

"We'd love that," Brodie says. "Can you teach me to make penguin? I love penguins."

"What's your phone number?" Rowen has picked up a crayon and a piece of paper.

"Rowen you can't just ask people for their phone numbers."

"Why not? We'll need to make arrangements."

She just looks at me expectantly. So, I slowly tell her my phone number. I try to remember age six. Can she even write my number down? Guess I'll find out.

I can't tell if he's teasing me. Doesn't matter. Because in the next moment Maise is throwing her arms around my waist.

"Thank you. Thank you so much." Her voice is quivering with emotion. It's such a small thing, but she's so happy. The other two throw their arms around me as well.

Tears start to well up in my eyes. *I've really got to*

get some sleep.

"I almost forgot. I brought you some treats." I tell them. "The boxes are on the coffee table."

Before I can get the whole sentence out the girls have run off. We hear happy squeals from the living room.

"Come on. We should go while they are distracted. If it were up to them, they would keep you here all day. You've got to get home and get some sleep."

He takes my hand, again, and starts to lead me to the library.

Chapter Nine

Callum

I've got to stop touching her. But I can't seem to help myself. Her hand in mine, it just feels right. Her in this house. Her with the girls, it all feels right. But it's not. The lass is twenty-two years old, and the owner of a thriving business. She's too young to date a man with three young girls. *Daughters*, my wolf chides me. *Call them by their true name. And the woman, she is our mate.* My wolf doesn't understand the intricacies of the modern world. Or the fact that twenty-two-year-old women are rarely ready to have a family, nowadays. I try to focus. Try to make myself let go of her hand. But I can't.

"It's clever. The first time I realized the book looked funny, I was eight. I started to pull it down and realized it was attached to the shelf. Then the door swung open. Gram says I screamed so loud, she thought I'd broken my arm."

She reaches up and starts to pull a leather-bound book which is not really a book, but a lever. Clever. Wolfs are always too clever. There's a creaking sound and the whir of a gear, and then a section of the library swings back, exposing a pitch-black tunnel.

"You used to play in here?"

"Yup. Grandma tried to forbid it, but I think my Grandpa realized I would do it anyway. How is a kid supposed to resist it? So, he got a flashlight and inspected it. Made sure all the hinges were oiled and doors worked. After he felt it was safe, he took me through it a half dozen times before he'd let me play in it alone. And then only if I had a flashlight, and I told them where I was going. Oh, I forgot to ask you if you had flashlights?"

Since my whole family can see in the dark that would be a no.

"Actually, I don't think we have any in the house. We should…"

"Oh, you know what? I've got a flashlight on my phone, so we are fine. You ready?"

She lets go of my hand, so she can fish her cellphone out of her pocket. She shakes it twice and a bright light turns on.

"You ready?"

She points the flashlight into the tunnel, then with her other hand she takes hold of mine. I feel like I've won the lottery. A feeling of joy spreads through my chest, and my wolf starts to laugh. I don't care. I just squeeze her hand tighter and let her lead the way.

The more we walk the tunnel the less I like the idea of any child playing in it. It seems like it would give a child nightmares. I tell her that and she laughs. Her laugh is a lovely thing, musical and warm.

"I used to love it in here. I'd sneak a Nancy Drew book in, with a bag of my grandpa's oatmeal cookies. And a glass of milk. I would hang out for hours. I felt like an explorer, you know. Like I discovered this secret space, and it was all mine. I used to hang my drawings on the wall with scotch tape. I wonder if they…"

Lily trips. I reach out to catch her before she can hit the ground. I grab her firmly by the waist and pull her up. Then I can't help it. I pull her close and wrap my arms around her. She smells like vanilla, and warm milk. Delicious. I breathe her in. I can hear her heart beating wildly in her chest.

"You're okay. I've got you." I whisper. I draw soothing circles on her back. Her heart is still pounding, and I can feel her tremble in my arms.

"Lily what's the matter?"

She doesn't answer. She presses up on her toes and wraps her tiny hand in my hair. Then she's pulling me close. She brushes her lips over mine, a barely there whisper of lips that's the sexiest thing I've ever felt. Then she growls, and her mouth meets mine. Her kisses are hungry, needy things. Like she can't get enough of me.

My wolf preens.

I pull my mouth away just for a moment. "What's the hurry, Luv" I whisper. She groans and tries to pull me closer.

She's such a tiny thing. I hold her steady.

"Shh, I want to savor this. I've dreamed of this."

I put my hands on her shoulders and start to kiss her properly. Slow, lingering kisses, first on her delicate collarbone, and up the gentle line of her neck. I kiss her softly, like her first brush of lips over mine. I take my time. Until she's making little needy cries in the back of her throat. Then I put my lips on hers and start to kiss. Thorough, learning kisses. I want to know what makes her moan. What makes her lean in closer? I tangle my hands in her hair. When I give it a tug, she groans 'yes' into my mouth. I pick her up so I can deepen the angle of our kisses. She wraps her little legs around me, and I cup my hand around her perfectly rounded ass. Every inch of this girl is perfect. Heart, mind, body. Perfect. Too perfect to pull into my messy life. Reluctantly, I start to soften the kisses. Then I pull away and gently put her back on her feet.

"Lily we shouldn't, we can't... I don't want to.... We should get back."

Chapter Ten

Lily

He doesn't want to what? Kiss me? I know I kissed him first, but he kissed me back. I know he wants me, at least physically. I could feel it. The want poured off him in waves. So, what is it? I'm not good enough for him? Well, you know what? He's not good enough for me. I deserve someone better than an evictor of Grandmas and I'm sure that's not the worst thing he's ever done. *Beautiful is as beautiful does.* My Grandpa always said that, and I'd do well to remember it. Just cause he's beautiful on the outside doesn't mean he's a nice guy on the inside and I deserve a nice man.

"Let's get this over with." I push ahead and keep the pace brisk. He tries to talk to me.

"Don't want to hear it, all right." I stomp ahead.

Once we make it to the attic, I open the door to the hall and start to race down the stairway.

"Hey Brodie!" I'm shouting and I don't even care. "Could you give me a ride home?"

Callum gives me a strange look, but he doesn't try to stop me. The girls are unaware of the drama. They want to know when I'm coming over.

"I don't know. Soon though." Shit. I just lied to three grieving girls. There's a special pit in hell for people who do that. Wait I'm probably the only person in the universe who's ever done that. Great a room in hell reserved for me alone.

"Wanna talk about it?" Brodie asks, when we're alone in his pickup truck.

"Uh no."

"I'm sure Cal did something stupid. I'm used to it. I'm his brother. You can tell me if you want to."

I wish I could. Talking to Brodie is easy. I wonder if this is what it's like talking to a brother. That would be nice. A brother, a big family. I guess we always want what we don't have. I almost tell him what happened, but I'm not that sleep deprived.

"It's complicated for Cal right now. You might not be seeing my brother at his best, but he really is a good man. Funny, smart, he could be better looking I know, but you shouldn't hold that against him. And when he loves, he loves with his whole heart."

"Good to know, but I think that's a little too much information, Brodie."

He insists on walking me to the door. Waiting until I find my keys. Then he gives me a hug.

"Pretty sure I'll be seeing you again. Get some sleep Lily."

****

I'm so tired, I don't even change out of my clothes. I just crawl into bed.

When I wake up my room is pitch black. And I'm hungry and cranky. I had Cal dreams. My psyche is weird. For some reason, I can't have normal sexy, sex dreams. For some reason Callum and I were in a forest. Nekkid. I was chasing him. Then I caught him, and things got good. Really good. Okay, I'm blushing. I have got to get a social life.

My phone says it's already four o'clock. I've slept most of the day away. Janie will be closing for the day. I hope she was okay. Sundays are a big day.

She answers on the third ring.

"Hey Rockstar? Wanna guess how many orders you have for abominable snowman cookies. Twelve special orders. I stopped taking requests because I thought you might kill me. Or worse make me try to help you bake. You know that never ends well. And Lois from the Phoenicia Daily News? She took some pictures of the window for the paper. Did you get some sleep?"

"I did. Did you have plans for dinner?"

"No. How about pizza?"

"Sounds great. Meet you in an hour?"

****

"Lily I'm serious, you've got to stop keeping the details out of your stories. He drove you home in complete silence. Not a word was spoken with that sexy accent of his? And he took you straight home, I suppose? You didn't go anywhere else? Like the local diner perhaps?"

"How did you. . .?"

"Gail Ferris saw you. You'll be happy to know she thinks he's too tall for you, and she has a nephew that would be a much better match. She left me his number. Would you like it? Now, I want details. You're going to tell me everything. She did say he has good manners. Helped you out of the booth and everything."

I take a bite of pizza and stalled for time. I'm dying to tell her the story, but the kissing feels personal. Sacred almost. I don't want to tell anyone and cheapen it. Not that it mattered at all to Callum. He probably kisses women all the time. Actually, I don't really think that.

Part of me thinks he dates as infrequently as I do, and that he was just as surprised by this attraction as I was. I wish I could understand why he pulled away.

Well, if you wanted to know what he was thinking you probably should have let him talk. Maybe. But I was angry. What with all the 'I shouldn't, I can't' stammering that he was doing. I decide to tell Janie the story without the kissing bits and see if she can make sense of it. Then my phone rings. It's an unfamiliar number, but I pick it up. I don't want to miss a call if it might be a special order.

"This is Lily."

"This is Rowen." I hear her giggle into the phone. "Do you always answer your phone like that."

"I do." I say suppressing my laugh. This cheeky girl is cracking me up.

"When are you coming over? We are all excited, especially Maisie."

"I'm not sure. I'm really busy at work."

"How about tomorrow? Your store is closed on Mondays. I looked it up. If you tell me what we need for cupcakes, Fiona could drive us to the store."

"Rowen why do you have my phone? Who are you talking to?"

"Hello? Who is this?" Another voice comes on the line.

"Hi, I'm Lily. I own the bakery is town. I met the girls today. I'm guessing you are Fiona."

"Hi, Lily. I am. Sorry about this. Rowen got a hold of my phone. Let me just walk into another room."

I hear footsteps and a door.

"Sorry. They were so excited to meet you, and you might have noticed Rowen has a take no prisoners kind of way about her. It's tricky, because I don't want to squash her sense of self, and they are in a strange country. It's hard. They went crazy for your little snowman cookies. Which I adored by the way. Especially the odd-looking ones in the kilts. Those were my personal favorites. Obviously, I would love to have you come over and bake with the kids. But there's no pressure. I know you must be busy."

"I am, I'd love to, but this is the holiday season and…."

"It's just that Maisie's stuck in the house for a while. It's hard when you are six. Your visit would mean the world to her, but I understand if you are too busy. You probably have plans for your day off."

I suddenly understand where Rowen learned to play hardball.

"I could probably find a couple hours tomorrow afternoon. If that worked for you?"

"Perfect. I'll get the supplies. Just tell me what you need."

"It's okay. I have a bakery. I can bring the supplies. No problem."

"Lily, I can't wait to meet you. Ro wants to say goodbye. Is that all right?"

"Of course."

"Guess what, Lily?"

"What?"

"After you left, we got a surprise. Well, two surprises. We got a swing set with a playhouse and two slides. The playhouse is going to be pink or maybe yellow but probably pink. And the best part. Uncle Brodie brought a puppy home. He's brown with spots, and his name is Mr. Bunny."

I want to ask about the name, but I don't.

"That's wonderful. I can't wait to meet him." I hear Fiona's voice. A low murmur in the background.

"Thank you for the cookies."

"You are welcome, Rowen. I'll see you tomorrow. Tell Fiona I'll come over around one, okay?"

"Okay."

Janie just looks at me with a huge grin.

"Spending a lot of time in the enemies lair."

"Janie, you have no idea."

Chapter Eleven

Callum

"Rowen did what?"

"Cal I've already explained this. Rowen took my phone. She called Lily. Pulled out the 'my poor sister can't leave the house card' and guilted the nice young woman into coming over. She should be here any moment."

"I can't believe you are telling me this now."

"Why?" My sister-In-Law has an evil grin on her face. "Did you want to change into a nicer shirt? You look fine, Cal."

"I thought we were going to make joint decisions where the girls were concerned."

"Cal, come on. We are talking about cookies."

"No, I do believe we are taking about cupcakes," my brother says. "Penguin cupcakes, I believe. You don't have to be here if you don't want to. Fiona and I have got this."

"You are not being fair to her. Making her come over like this."

"You're sure we are the ones not being fair to her?" Fi asks.

I'm about to growl my answer when the doorbell rings.

"We've got it!" The girls come flying down the

stairs. The pup they insisted on calling Mr. Bunny comes running down the stairs behind them.

"Whoa. Just one moment."

I wait till all eyes are on me.

"If you start to feel like you need to shift, even if you are having a great time and don't want to leave, you need to tell me. So, we can go outside and run it off. All right, Maisie Daisy. The girls will come with us, so you don't miss anything." Rowen looks like she wants to object but I give her a look.

"We'll come with you, Maise." She gives her sister a hug.

"Okay."

"All right. Go answer the door then." They run off with Fi and the pup behind them.

"Do you think this will work?" I ask my brother.

"I do. They already know her. And Maisie's getting better control. She must socialize sometime. And if she did shift it's much easier to wipe the memory of one human than twenty. Never pleasant that."

"I don't want to wipe anyone's memory."

"Well, it probably won't come to that. Also, it's possible that Lily might be someone to trust with our secret."

Now he's just being ridiculous. The only humans who know our secrets are our mates.

I hear the girls greet her. The sounds of hugs and kisses. Fi taking her coat. Lilly admiring Mr. Bunny. The girls come in carrying the supplies, and then Fiona comes in with Lily.

Exhausted, Lily is a beautiful woman. But with a good night's sleep she is radiant. She's arranged her curls in a braid that she's wrapped around her head like a crown. She looks like a fierce warrior princess. She's wearing a simple blush colored sweater that's pushed up around her elbows exposing her delicate tattoo blossoms. Her beautiful bottom is tucked nicely into a pair of skinny jeans. It's hard to look away. I wasn't planning on staying. I'll be nearby if Maisie needs me, but I wasn't going to torture myself with an afternoon of the woman I want but can't have.

That is until she walks past me and mutters in a low voice pitched just for me: "I didn't think you'd be here."

I find myself taking the box out of her hands and following her into the kitchen like I was a young pup.

She's wonderful with the girls, just like I thought she would be. She's pre-baked the cupcakes. She lets the girls make the buttercream and shows them how to make basic shapes with the fondant. And how to stick the pieces together with water.

Rowen and Katie's creations look like a kid made them. So does my cat, although Brodies penguin is rather good. Maisie's is the best of the bunch. She may turn out to be an artist. Her fondant rendition of Mr. Bunny is spot on. Her wolf has not stirred once. Which is a wonderful thing. I exclaim over all the girl's creations. Cupcakes are devoured and all too soon Lily is saying her goodbyes.

The girls insist on putting on their coats and hats, so they can walk Lily out. The whole family follows her to her car. Even Mr. Bunny is pressed against Maisie's chest.

Lily parked her car on the edge of the driveway like she was prepared for a quick getaway. I'll have to find a way to apologize to her. I'm so fixed on her I don't notice Mr. Bunny growing restless.

He's so quick, he's a blur. Jumping out of Maisie's arms and running toward the road. The road full of cars driving faster than they should. *The girls cannot lose anyone else.* That's the only thought in my head and then instinct takes over, and I start to turn. I don't think about it until it's too late. I've already shifted into my wolf and bound out of the driveway and into the road. I manage to grab the pup carefully by the scruff of his neck before he's hit by a car. I see Brodie take Lily by the arm and steer her toward the house. My wolf wants to knock him to the ground, but I force my thoughts to clear. He's keeping the girls safe, I tell my wolf. The pup whimpers and squeals but I don't release him until I'm safely through door, and Fiona has locked it. Everyone watches me in silence. I drop the pup and walk up the stairs to shift.

What the hell have I done? I let the turn wash over me. In moments I'm naked on my hardwood floor. *Stupid, bloody, idiot.* I pull on a fresh shirt and jeans. I could sit in this room and pretend nothing happened, but I don't have that luxury, so I force myself down the stairs. Will there be a look of revulsion on her beautiful face, or a look of fear?

When I reach the bottom of the stairs, I realize she just looks angry.

"Are you out of your mind? You ran into traffic. You could have been hit by a car."

I look closer, and I realize the only emotion on her beautiful face is loving concern. In that moment I know exactly what I'm going to do.

"Fiona, Brodie would you take the girls upstairs please."

Maisie steps in front of Lily.

144

"No. If you wipe her memory, she'll forget us. I don't want her to forget about us."

"Is that what you? You can do that? Oh hell no." For a human she's fast. She's through the door in a moment and running through the snow. She may be quick, but I know I'm faster.

"Maisie Daisy you have my word everything's going to be fine."

I pull on my boots, and then I start to run.

My wolf loves any chase, but this is special, sacred. Chasing our mate.

Mine my wolf cries and this time I don't disagree. She doesn't head for the car. She continues through the snow. When I see her pull her cellphone out, I realize it's time to stop the chase.

I catch her around the waist, as gently as I can. I make sure my body takes the weight of the fall. I pull her securely on top of me.

"Let go of me. Leave me alone."

"You can't run from my wolf, Luv. It's always going to catch you."

"I can't believe you think you are going to wipe my memory. What gives you the right to mess with my mind?"

It's probably not a good idea to tell her that righteous indignation makes her look more beautiful. Her cheeks are flushed. Her curls have tumbled around her face. She'll look like this in my bed. But better, she'll look sated. I want nothing more than to kiss her senseless, but we need to have a chat.

"Why do you think I'd take your memories?"

"Because Maisie said so. Because I saw you…"

"She's a six-year-old girl, Lily. And I'm a selfish

man. Who hates the idea that you wouldn't remember him. I want you thinking about me. I'd love it if your thoughts were consumed by me. Like I'm consumed by thoughts of you. I want you, Lil. But you're young and I don't come alone. If you choose me, you choose the whole package. You need to make sure this is what you want. Could you see your life like this? With us? You need to think on it. Whatever you decide, your memories are safe. I trust you with my life. More importantly I trust you with theirs."

And then because I'll use every weapon in my arsenal, I proceed to kiss her senseless.

Chapter Twelve

Lily

You know when people say, 'Boy, did I have a day.' Well, I just had a day. And I can't tell anyone about it. But there's someone I need to talk to. Someone who needs to know.

"Grandma?"

"Honey, are you all right? You sound a little funny."

"I think I might be in love…."

One Year later
Christmas Eve

"Honey, they're perfect. Thank you so much." The girls hand me the cake toppers, and I sit them gently on the cake. I guess most women wouldn't bake their own wedding cake. But what can I say? I know what I want. And the girls helped. We decided to make a six-layer white chocolate grapefruit cake with a white chocolate ganache. Maisie made the cake toppers. A splendid wolf shaped bride and groom in beautiful fondant finery. Most people will just think they are dogs, and we are big dog people. That's okay. Those people that know will know. Right alongside the wolfie bride and groom are three little pups in little pink dresses, and flower garlands. Perfect. Callum walks into the room.

"Only you would be fussing with the wedding cake

on your Wedding day."

"I wanted to see it one more time."

"It's perfect, and so are you. You ready my love?"

I'm probably not ready for everything that life will throw my way, but I know that I love this man and these three little girls, my daughters, with all my heart. And that in the end, love is enough.

Luring the Lykan with Almond Macarons

by

Leslie Ann Brown

Christmas Cookies Series

"Okay, Jo, I officially confess to being lost in the Canadian wilderness," announced Nicky, my satyr chauffer. I raised my eyebrow at him and made no comment. We were driving through a lovely little town, all dressed up for Christmas with inflatable characters on front lawns and garland wrapped around porch pillars. It had snowed recently, but only a dusting covered the brown grass.

"I think you exaggerate, Nicky. Where are those instructions you printed out?" After three days travelling from Florida, the luxury SUV's interior was a mess due to Nicky's insistence on buying souvenirs every time we stopped to eat or sleep. I twisted in my seat to look behind and saw the dog-eared corners of the sheaf of directions sticking out from underneath a red sweatshirt bearing the declaration that the wearer loved Canada. I snagged the papers and leafed through to the last page. I frowned.

"The directions end with this town. We're supposed to punch some numbers into a GPS, whatever that is."

"Jo, you know darn well what a GPS is. It's been sitting in front of you on my dash for the whole trip. Punch the numbers in." Nicky pulled the SUV over in front of a store front whose window announced that hunting and fishing licenses were for sale within. I pointedly handed him the page with the information on it.

"You know I don't do that kind of thing."

"For the sake of the vanished gods, Jo!" gritted Nicky. I peeked and saw that his usually sunny yellow aura was turning muddy.

I was surprised. Nicky had been a pleasant travelling companion up until now, putting up with my

151

technophobia. His handsome face with the stereotypic goatee was creased with annoyance. So now Nicky was tired of me, just like my Grove sisters. He had been delighted with the assignment to drive me to my new job in Northern Ontario when we were in Florida. "Road trip!" he had caroled and then told me to ignore the permanent tent in his pants that all satyrs sported. He would be the perfect gentleman. This was very un-satyr-like behavior, so I wondered if one of my Grove sisters had told him to leave me alone. If so, it was another example of them coddling me, even as they were forcing me out of the Grove. They didn't think I could handle it on my own, that I was too fragile. Still, I liked Nicky and tried to smooth things over.

"Why are you angry with me, Nicky? It's not my intention to be obstinate."

He sighed and rubbed the spot where his horns were hidden in his luxuriant chestnut head of hair. "I'm not mad, Jo. I just don't get you. If I had been in a healing sleep in my tree for seventy years, the first thing I'd do upon emerging would be to get up to speed with the new century. There're so many advancements that have made the world a much smaller place. Humans have been to the moon, for Dionysus's sake. And yet, you make a point of avoiding it all. You haven't struck me as being an unreasonably stubborn person, so why, Honey Lips?"

It was complicated to say the least, and I hadn't even begun to unravel all my reasons for myself, let alone be able to explain it to others. I looked at my clenched hands resting in my lap. "I don't know, Nicky. One minute I was going to blow up some train tracks with my French Resistance cell, and the next it was all fire and bullets. Then my tree is disgorging me onto the grass in the

Florida Grove. It was horrifying to find out that I had been so badly hurt that it took seventy years to heal me, first in a loaned tree in Provence and then in my own tree. Every human I knew was long dead." I glanced at him but saw nothing but sympathy. "You know I had a human lover, yes?"

Nicky nodded. "Yes. He was a baker in a family of bakers in the Montmartre district of Paris. You joined the Resistance together, and he died in the same ambush that injured you."

I looked back down at my hands. "I miss him. I miss the life we had in the bakery before the war. Those were happy times, and it would have been years before he would have noticed I wasn't aging. But that was all snatched away from me. My sisters in the Grove want me to forget about what I've lost and get with the program. Apparently, I have too much potential to waste my time moping around the Grove. This assignment is to start me on the path to reintegrating with society but…"

"You haven't finished grieving." Nicky's sympathy made me want to burst into tears.

"No, not yet. I've been outside of my tree for two years now, so I do understand that I have to move on, but it's all too much." It made me feel weak and cowardly. Where was the courage I had dredged up when we fought the Nazis? I had been a fearless warrior. Now I lived in the shadows, pulling a corner of my shawl over my face, hiding. I was startled out of my thoughts by a gentle hand on my knee.

"Jo, take your time. Grief doesn't have a schedule. Going to this the lykán camp will be good for you. You can integrate back in at your own pace."

I sat up straighter. "Sure, Nicky. Let's do this GPS

thing."

Nicky ended up punching in the numbers, but I watched him do it. I jumped a little when the box on the dashboard spoke in the sultry tones of a woman with a British accent.

"Drive 2.4 miles along County Road 19 to the intersection of Regional Road 12."

"And we're off!" declared Nicky.

****

After numerous twists and turns, we pulled up to iron gates. I squinted up at name carved into the wooden sign that hung above me.

Dyre Private Resort

I shook my head. How subtle. I let out a long sigh.

"More second thoughts, Jo? Courage, Honey Lips."

I smiled at Nicky. I would be sorry to see him leave, but he was needed in Michigan for something or other. Fortunately, I would have Aunt Min to keep me company at Camp Dyrewolf.

"Always, Nicky. But I'm looking forward to seeing Aunt Min. She counseled me for a few months after I left my tree but then she had to leave for this job."

An intercom on the gate pillar on Nicky's side crackled. "You going to tell me who you are or just sit there all day?" It was a testy, male voice.

I looked up and saw a camera.

Nicky leaned toward the intercom. "Nicolas Andropopulis delivering Joanna Kourakis."

"Yeah." I heard the click as the intercom turned off. I pushed the button to roll down my window. Despite the chill in the air, I stuck my head out and inhaled the scent of the pine forest. I missed the company of trees. As I did hundreds of times a day, I reached up to finger the polished disc of wood hanging from its leather thong around my neck. It was from my tree and allowed me to leave my Grove without sickening and dying.

I sensed him rather than saw him. Turning my head slowly to the right, I locked gazes with a slender white wolf with amber eyes. My first *lykánthropos*, and he was magnificent. An adolescent by the looks of him, with legs that were too gangly and shoulders that were too narrow. I wondered how much effort it would take for him to launch into the air and fly through the window at my throat. One snap of his jaws, and my hundred-year-long life would be over.

"Bring it on, fluffy," I told him. Nicky's head jerked toward me, and he saw the lykán. He cursed under his breath. There was no love lost between Pan's get and the children of Selene.

The wolf gave me a big doggy smile and lifted a leg. A copious stream of urine marked the SUV's back tire.

"You can piss on it all you like, it's still *my* sweet ride." Nicky was furious underneath his insouciant reply. He had explained to me exactly how much the top-of-the-line SUV had cost him. I was still baffled by modern prices. For what he had paid for the large chunk of rolling metal, Armand and I could have bought three bakeries in Paris.

With a flick of his tail, the wolf shifter vanished into the thick pines. The gates started to swing open. They looked on the verge of falling apart from rust, but the hinges made no sound as they moved. The veneer of neglect over very efficient machinery. I had done some studying of lyk*á*ns when I found out I was to come here and knew that was a common lykán ruse.

We drove up the dirt road through heavy forest.

Frozen weeds stuck up in the center and brushed the undercarriage, but there were no potholes, washouts, or washboards. Again, care under apparent neglect. As we rounded a long curve, the resort appeared before us. Rustic would be one word to describe it. The buildings were made from logs and painted rust red. The end of each log was tipped with white for variety. We pulled up in front of a sign that said, "Guests Only".

The screen door opened, and Aunt Min bustled out, carrying a suitcase. As expected, she looked no different from the last time I had seen her: pale blonde hair done up in a chignon, merry chocolate brown eyes and the physical appearance of a human woman in her late forties although she was hundreds of years older than that. Physically, I was very similar to her, being from the same Grove lineage, although to human eyes I appeared to be twenty years younger. Never the fashion plate, Aunt Min wore shapeless cargo pants and a puffy pink down-filled parka zipped up to her neck. She held a steaming coffee cup decorated with a picture of a mosquito and the caption "Nipigon Air Force".

"Jo and Nicky! Right on time. Unload your belongings, dear. I'm in a hurry."

I slowly got out of the SUV and watched Aunt Min throw her suitcase carelessly into Nicky's back seat. It landed on a pile of ceramic souvenirs, and I heard something break. Nicky gave a wordless yelp and darted around to the back hatch to remove my two bags. Keeping one eye on Aunt Min, he placed them on the porch. He gave me a sideways hug so I wouldn't get poked by his happy stick and then leapt back into the driver's seat.

"Aunt Min?" That was plaintive even to my own

ears.

She gave me a quick hug and plopped herself into what had been my seat. "I'm in a rush, dear. Kel will look after you. Have fun." She reached over and squeezed the satyr's thigh. "I know I will. Nicky, let's go." The look on Nicky's face was priceless. The satyr might have met his match.

I stood there forlornly watching Nicky back into the parking lot and do a quick turnabout. The last glimpse I had of Aunt Min was of her waving out her window. Her tinkling laugh echoed through the tall pines. I had been looking forward to spending time with the one Grove sister who didn't get on my case about my Luddite tendencies. It never occurred to me that I was Min's replacement. The screen door thumped again, and I turned to see a man emerge from the building's dark interior.

His aura told me he was lykán since I had never seen that boiling orange color in a human. The man's approach, all smooth and deadly predator, confirmed my guess. He leaned against one of the support pillars for the porch's roof and gave me the once over. He seemed less than impressed.

I gave a little wave. "I'm Joanna Kourakis, but most people call me Jo."

"Jo." He tasted the name and found it sour. This must be the Kel who was to look after me. Kel was dark and lean, with wide shoulders. The amber eyes above the beard stubble must be a lykán characteristic. "You're replacing Minerva as our healer, I take it."

Ooh, nobody called Min "Minerva". I gave a smile that was more of a wince. "I wasn't aware that she would be leaving. This has really taken me by surprise. I'm not sure I'm prepared to take over here."

"Oh, you wouldn't be taking over. The Lykán Conclave grudgingly lets this place exist, and one of their stipulations is that we have an empathic healer on call." Kel leaned forward and lowered his voice but my dryad hearing picked up his words perfectly well. "But nobody will be calling you." Kel did snark well.

"Well, super. Glad to know I'll be able to meet expectations." I was stranded here now with no apparent way of leaving and no job to do.

"Yeah, not big on expectations here." Now he was being smug. "I'm Kel Hawthorne. I'll get your cabin key." He ducked back into the office, and, although I hadn't been invited, I followed him.

I was surprised to find myself in a charming lobby. There were brochures for local attractions and a topographic map of the area on the wall behind the reception counter. Homemade posters advertised events such as Christmas in July and the Great Scavenger Hunt. I felt Kel's gaze on me.

"Is this all window dressing?" I asked, waving my hand at the lobby.

"Yeah. Some humans do make it up here, despite the gate. Or they motor across the lake. They're told this place is private membership only, and most leave without a fuss." He selected from a wall rack one of a dozen large antique keys that had numbers hanging from them. The one he selected was number five. I wondered what happened to the humans who did make a fuss.

Kel pushed by me and exited without holding the screen door open for me. I caught it with my foot before it could slam in my face. Walking by my two lonely bags in the parking lot, he headed up a dirt road that ran up a hill beside the lodge. Sighing, I picked up the bags and followed him.

I hadn't quite caught up to him by the time he strode up onto the porch of a sweet little cabin and fitted the key to the front door. I followed him inside and surveyed the contents of the cabin with approval. There was a kitchen complete with stove and refrigerator. A comfy sofa and matching armchair faced a stone fireplace.

Kel opened a door. "Your bedroom. Bathroom is next door. I've stocked you with towels, but you're in charge of laundering them."

"No maid service then?" I said jokingly and was rewarded with a frown.

"Everyone here cleans up after themselves. Or at least those who wear skin occasionally. The ones who stay in fur don't need to worry about it."

"How many are there of each category?" I was curious as to how many patients I might have. Kel told me they wouldn't be needing my services, but it wouldn't hurt to know.

"You don't need to know that," he answered, unsurprisingly.

"Okay." I put my suitcases down by the bedroom door. Going to the kitchen, I checked the contents of the refrigerator and then started opening cupboards. I was well stocked for now, but no doubt I was expected to rustle up my own supplies in the future. I could feel Kel hovering behind me. I couldn't trust my empathic senses with an unfamiliar species, but he felt a little off balance to me. Was my apparent lack of despair at being unwanted throwing him off?

"There's enough food to last you a couple of days. I bought you the same stuff Minerva ate. I make a grocery run every Monday morning. Make a list of what you want. Leave it at the office. Or you can email it to me."

I turned to face him. "I don't do email. I'll drop the list off at the front desk."

He smirked. "Not at all? Don't even want to know what the Wi-Fi password is?"

"Nope." Agape, leader of the Florida Grove dryads, had pressed one of those little phones on me when I left. It was at the bottom of one of the suitcases.

Kel crossed his arms. "You're a strange one. Not anything like Minerva."

I smiled. "You have that correct. You leave me alone, and I'll leave you alone. And everyone is happy. Is there anything else you wish to show me?" *If not, leave*.

"No." He subjected me to his amber stare a few seconds too long, obviously debating whether to say something else. He gave into the impulse. "Keep out of the woods. The ones who stay in fur can be impulsive."

I cocked my head to one side. "You're telling a dryad to stay out of the woods? Did that work with Min?"

"No, but she could take care of herself."

My shoulders tensed. "And I can't?"

His shoulders shrugged. "I don't know. There's something about you. Something lost. Or sad. It makes you seem like prey."

I laughed. "Does 'impulsive' translate to 'hunt down and eat lone dryads found in the woods'? Do I need to carry some sort of protection? Like wolfsbane? A rolled-up newspaper?"

"You can try, but I wouldn't recommend it. Enjoy your cabin." He extended the key to me, and I took it. He left, gently closing the door behind him. I hovered there for a moment and then locked it. I didn't feel threatened here, but I wouldn't ignore Kel's warning about impulsive campers who never changed out of their wolf form.

I found a glass in one of the cupboards and ran the sink water before filling it. The water tasted pure, free of the chemicals the cities put in their water supplies. In Florida, we either drank rainwater or bought (!) spring water tasting of the plastic it was bottled in. I had found a good thing about this place already. I could be positive if I put my mind to it.

My bedroom had a comfy double bed and a dresser set. I unpacked my belongings and stowed my suitcases under the bed. I found the phone and placed it on the top of the dresser. It dinged at me, and I ignored it. The bathroom had a glass-walled shower on one side and a free-standing tub on the other. Again, luxury hidden in a rustic setting. Exploring further, I found a mud room at the back of the cabin and a door that led to a deck. I slipped my coat back on to check it out.

There was a little clearing ringed with poplars and maples. There must have been a fire within the last twenty years to explain the lack of spruce and pine. Or it had been cleared to build the resort. I would commune with the soil later and try and find out the wood's history. There was a rustle in the undergrowth to my right, and I turned to face the sound. The adolescent white wolf emerged from the foliage and stood there panting a grin at me.

"We meet again," I commented. The wolf rippled as if in a heat mirage. A teenager stood there, naked, but he politely covered his bits with his hands. One of those who wore skin on occasion, then. He was a good-looking kid with reddish-blonde hair that contrasted nicely with his amber eyes.

"Hi," he said. "I'm Evan."

"Joanna but you can call me Jo."

"What if I want to call you Anna? Or Anna-Jo?" His grin was sly.

"I can't stop you, but I may not answer to it." I touched his mind with my empathic abilities. I felt what I thought was curiosity and a bit of male interest. He was a teenager after all. "You visiting, Evan? Perhaps you could bring clothes next time."

"Arcadians aren't bothered much by nudity. Are dryads different? Prudish maybe?"

I ignored his innuendos. "Arcadians? Is that what you call yourselves? I've been using lyk*á*n in my mind. Was that rude?"

Evan pursed his lips. "Not really, I guess. It's just not something we call ourselves. We originated in Arcadia, Greece."

"Well, I'll try and call you Arcadians from now on. Do you want to come in? I can lend you some sweatpants."

"Why do you keep trying to dress me, Anna-Jo?"

"As your counselor, it would not be appropriate to be alone with you when you have no clothes on. Plus, you must be freezing."

He appeared to consider that, and then his mocking grin broke out again. "But I don't need a counselor, so I'll pass on the invite. And I don't feel the cold that much. Have a nice day, Anna-Jo."

"You too, Evan." I watched as he shimmered back into a wolf. With a flick of his tail, he melted into the woods. I knew he would be back. His attraction to me was superficial, but his curiosity was not.

****

There was a bookshelf in my cabin. It held what I assumed was typical fare for a cottage visitor. There were books on tree and bird identification, as well as on local history. There was a large stock of romances, and I noted with amusement that one was entitled *The Dryad's Lost Love*. I pulled it off the shelf, and an envelope fell to the floor. I picked it up and saw it was addressed to me.

I opened it and went right to the final signature. As I suspected, it was from Aunt Min. I sighed and made myself comfortable on the sofa.

Dear Jo,

Surprise! You're here and I'm not. But, as we both know, I couldn't do anything for you two years ago so why should it be any different now? There was talk at the Grove of shipping you to the Greek colony, so I put the kibosh on that by telling them to send you here. I think you'll benefit from not having a sister ask you how you are doing every five minutes and from having something to take your mind off things. Kel will tell you that there's nothing for you to do here but you've already figured out that's not true.

There are thirty shifters here, including Kel. Of those, all are adolescent, except Kel. seventeen never shift to human form. Of the twelve that do, only about five are interested in interaction. The others shift so that they can eat human food when they tire of wild game. They all have their reasons for preferring wolf form but won't talk to you about it. In the past, the clans would have let them live their lives as wolves in some remote area, but modern civilization makes that difficult. There's always the risk that they might give away the existence of shifters. Hence this rehabilitation camp. It's only a few years old so Kel has a bit of time before the oldest kids reach adulthood and must conform to clan rules. Whether he admits it or not, he needs our help to find a solution that is acceptable to the Conclave.

Good luck, Kiddo and don't forget to have fun.
Your Auntie Min.
P.S. In case it's not obvious, burn after reading.

I read the letter again and then tossed it into the fire. It sounded like Kel had his work cut out for him. With so much at stake, I needed to find a way to reach the lykán adolescents. My empathic abilities were a bit better than Min's so hopefully I could push through where she couldn't. Sighing, I opened the dryad romance and settled in. Seems I had work to do after all, but I was going to have a little holiday first.

****

By the next morning, the temperature had dropped considerably. A cold wind stirred leafless branches, and the threat of snow loomed over me in the gray sky. I did have clothing for the occasion, not easily obtained in Florida, I might add. I bundled up warmly and took to the woods. There were clear trails in the snow, but I saw deer hoof rather than wolf pad prints. I jogged along at a good pace and congratulated myself for all the hard work I had put in to rehabilitate my body after its long sleep. I had to keep up the exercise so staying in my cabin was not for me. I would have to take my chances with the more impulsive lykáns. If things got a bit tense, I could slip into one of the big white pines dotting the trails.

There was a flash of white in the woods. Evan was

paralleling me. He had shown himself to be friendly, so I would assume he was escorting rather than stalking me. I got a bit worried when a larger, more formidable gray wolf joined him. If that big bruiser attacked, Evan wouldn't be able to stop him. I reached out mentally toward them to get the lay of the land. Evan wasn't thinking about much except the enjoyment of stretching his legs in a wood where all the brambles and bushes had died off in the cold weather. Passage was a lot easier. The other…I drew back quickly. It was Kel and he was angry. Of course. I was disobeying his instructions to stay out of the woods. Still, he was letting me go on my way, rather than forcing me to turn back.

More barely visible forms joined Evan and Kel. I had a full pack escort. I kept going for another hour, and no one bothered me. Some wolves dropped out and streaked away. New ones would join. At the end of my allotted time, I turned back, following my tracks to avoid getting lost. The last thing I wanted to do was ask Kel to lead me home. I reached my cabin door finally, pleasantly exhausted. My outing had served its purpose. I had gotten much needed exercise, I had shown Kel that I wasn't going to dance to his tune, and I had introduced myself to some of Camp Dyre's residents.

Once inside, I peeled off my boots and socks, and my coat, then padded over to the tamped-down fire and built it up. I made myself instant hot chocolate, promising myself that I would take the time in the future to heat milk on the stove for a proper version. Armand's mother, Madame Chenier, would have been horrified to see me making it in such a cavalier manner. I imagined her exclaiming in horror and pouring my cup down the drain. *Let me show you how it's done, my dear child.* She

165

had still had the soft accents of Provence even though she had been living in Paris for twenty years when I met her. I thought of the bakery with its rich warm smells, especially just before Christmas when we were all madly bustling to fill orders. It was hard work, but I had felt part of a family and proud that I could help.

The fire was burning nicely so I pulled the sofa closer and positioned the footstool in front of the fire. I was toasting my feet and sipping my inferior drink when there came a banging at my door. I cast out mentally. Kel. In a pissy mood.

"Come in," I called.

The door swung open forcefully, but Kel caught it before it hit the wall. He closed it and made a point of locking it.

"Sorry, forgot," I told him. "Country living and all that. But people do seem to knock before storming in."

"Why the hell did you ignore my advice and go for a skip in the woods?" he snarled at me. Literally. Then he sniffed the air in the direction of my hot chocolate.

"It wasn't a skip. It was a steady trot. I thought I had clearly indicated that I wasn't going to stay inside by my use of sarcasm."

Ignoring my response, Kel took off his boots and jacket and stomped over to my kitchenette.

"Hot chocolate is in the cupboard over the stove," I called without looking around.

"I know. I stocked your kitchen."

The water in the kettle was still hot so it wasn't long before he was back, flopping into the sofa's companion armchair. He nodded at the footstool. "Move."

I obediently shifted my feet over, and Kel thunked his size fourteens next to my size nines.

Kel cleared his throat. "So, let's discuss some rules."

"Sure." I could discuss as much as he wanted.

"If you have to go outside for walks, you do it with an escort."

"Okay," I said agreeably. It wasn't as if I could stop wolves from following me.

"You carry your phone with you at all times."

"Nope. Not doing that."

"Jo."

"Kel."

He scrubbed his hand over his face. "Why this resistance? It's a simple precaution to keep you safe."

I finished my hot chocolate before answering and looked around for a place to put the cup down. Kel took it from me and put it on the floor. I took a moment to organize my thoughts. "I don't want to be tied to it, the way I see people are now. If I can't get out of trouble with my own wits and dryad abilities, I can't see how calling for help is going to make a difference."

"A big shifter would make a difference."

"Is that what you call yourself? Evan told me you used the term Arcadians."

He finished his hot chocolate and put his cup next to mine. I had better remember to pick them up and wash them or I'd have a mouse problem. "When did you talk to Evan?"

"The first day I got here. Why? Is it not allowed?"

Kel shrugged. "If Evan wanted to talk to you, nothing wrong with that. But he was pulling your leg about us calling ourselves Arcadians. Only the stuffiest on the Conclave's ruling council use that term. What's that you wear around your neck?"

I went with his obvious change of subject. "My tree

167

or part of it. It lets me leave my Grove."

He leaned forward to touch it, and I clasped my hand around it. "Please don't. That's very intimate thing to do, and you were not invited." He sat back in his chair hands outspread in mock apology.

"What happens if you lose it, or it's taken away from you?"

It was my turn to shrug, not really wanting to answer but very aware that I needed to establish a rapport with this man. "I live for a while. If I can get back to my Grove and my tree, I will survive. If not, I wither and die. Then my tree does the same in the Grove. No trace of me left. Bye, bye Jo,"

He cocked his head at me. Perhaps I had slipped up, let something show in my tone.

"It sounds like you don't think that's an entirely bad thing. Have you been alive for so many centuries that you tire of life now?"

"Not at all. I'm young for a dryad, born in 1910 but my tree was planted in 1870." I saw his puzzlement and continued. "When dryads want to add to their numbers, there's a ceremony and a branch is taken from an existing tree. It's placed in the ground and grows for several years before a dryad forms inside and finally emerges. That's how dryads came to North America. A small group of Greek dryads brought branches donated from the Grove on Mykonos. They planted them and watched over them until their daughters emerged. Then they went home to Greece, leaving my sisters to make their own way in the New World."

"How long ago was that?" Kel had forgotten that I had never answered his question about being tired of life.

"They sailed with Ponce de León on his second visit

to Florida. They were hidden in the planks and masts. He never knew they were there."

"Can you do that? Hide in the walls?"

I frowned at him, wondering why he was asking. "Yes, but I'm out of practice."

"Do me a favor?"

"If I can." What on earth was he going to ask? I hadn't reached out empathically to him because he deserved his privacy, but it was all I could do not to scan him now.

"Practice."

"Practice what? Hiding in the walls?"

"Yes." He heaved himself out of the chair. "You might need to someday, and it would be comforting to know you were safe."

I blinked up at him, confused. Min had mentioned that Kel was keeping the teenagers safe, but there had been no indication of immediate danger. "Am I in danger here?"

"Not from us. But there are factions who would like to see the residents of Camp Dyre dealt with in a more permanent fashion. I wouldn't want you to be a casualty in that war."

"Me neither," I murmured. "But I won't hide in walls while you and the kids fight for your lives. That's not who I am."

Kel didn't answer me as he put his coat and boots back on. He paused with his hand on the doorknob. "I think I'm interested in finding out who you are, Jo Kourakis."

I almost laughed aloud. He said it so grudgingly, as if it was one the worst ideas he had had all year. And I couldn't ignore the little frisson of excitement his interest gave me. I turned the laugh into a smile. "I'm here for a while."

He frowned but not at me. "I just remembered. Your sister Agape called me this morning. She says she didn't give you a phone just to ignore it. She wants you to read your texts and emails. Also, she wants you to pick up when she calls. I'd rather she not call me anymore so throw her a bone, would you? Because she is not a pleasant person."

"I really have no clue how to use that thing. She'll have to write me a letter."

"A letter."

"You know, with pen and paper. And an envelope?"

He flashed me a smile that was all teeth. "I know what a letter is, but I bet none of the kids at this camp do. One of them can show you how to use your phone, Monday, at dinner."

"Dinner?"

"Mondays are spaghetti and meatballs night at the lodge. Be there at six or there won't be any left for you. And bring your phone."

After delivering his orders, Kel left, and I shuddered at the blast of cold air that came from that quick opening and closing of the door. I snuggled deeper into the sofa. Tomorrow was Sunday and I was going to laze around, writing up my grocery list. If I was invited to a dinner, I should bring a dessert. It was three weeks until Christmas, and my thoughts kept going back to happier times in Armand's bakery. Madame Chenier always gave me the almond macarons to make because she knew they were my favorite. I could start with those. Just the anticipation of baking made me feel as if I was exercising a muscle that was long atrophied. Painful at first but once you got going, it felt good. The other thing that felt good was the heat in Kel's amber eyes when he said he would like to know me better. I just wasn't sure that was a muscle I wanted to stretch.

****

I had slept well my first night at the camp. Maybe it was the cold Canadian air. But tonight, my past all came back with a vengeance. While my healing sleep in the tree had been dreamless, in the two years I had been back in the world, I spent a lot of nights dreaming what I called the fire dream.

It had been so quiet that night. The ten of us crept along the embankment that supported the railway track. Before we got to the holes we had dug in the slope for our explosives, a shot rang out in the dark accompanied with a curse in German. One of the ambushers had jumped the gun, but it didn't matter. The bullet hit the explosives Raoul was carrying, and we all went up like a string of roman candles. Armand turned to me, just before he died, his narrow, handsome face mirroring his despair. I hadn't died outright because I was at the end of the line and had time to throw my bundle of dynamite away from me. I was knocked unconscious and slept through my incarceration in a Gestapo jail, my rescue by the French dryads, and being slipped into a French Grove tree lent by a sister. It hadn't been ideal, but it kept me alive until they could arrange for my return to Florida after the war.

But in my repeating dream, I was awake and wading into the flames looking for Armand. I called and called but I knew he was gone, leaving me alone. I usually woke up desperately searching the bed for his body, and this was the case this time as well. Through my window,

171

I could see it was still dark with the moon just setting. Sitting up, I scrubbed my hands up and down my face. My throat was sore from yelling, and I took a swig of the ever-present glass of water on my nightstand. A howl echoed through the night, as lonely as I had been in my dream.

"Please don't come and check on me," I whispered to the distant singer. I didn't want to have to explain anything to anyone. My Grove sisters had grown tired of my issues, so I needed to keep them to myself here. I was getting better, incrementally. I just needed more time.

I couldn't get to sleep after that, so it was with bleary eyes that I walked down the hill to the lodge to deliver my grocery list, an hour after dawn. I had hoped to be able to leave it on the office counter but as soon as the bell above the door rang, Kel was out of the back room. He held his hand out for the list, and I plunked it on his palm.

He scanned it and frowned more deeply than his default position frown. "You want to bake?"

"Sure. Why not?"

"No one here is a big fan of sweets. Apex predators, you know."

I rolled my eyes. "Says the guy who stole my hot chocolate. All the more for me, then."

He folded the list and put it in his shirt pocket. He was wearing a different color of plaid flannel shirt today with black jeans. He snatched some keys from the counter. "You were just in time. I was about to drive up to your cabin to get your list."

"Can I come with you? I'd like to see what the grocery store carries." I wanted to get a sense of the community we lived near. Nicky had blasted through it, and I had to warn him about police and tickets.

"No. I'm the only one who goes into town."

It was my turn to frown. "That's a bit dictatorial. Are we prisoners here?"

Kel had come out from behind the counter, and I was reminded of the difference in our heights. The top of my head barely reached his collarbone. "It's safer. I don't want observers getting our measure. And I definitely don't want them scoping out our pretty little dryad. I'm the face of Camp Dyre to the public."

I ignored the throw away compliment. "I'm confused now. Are these observers from the anti-Dyre shifter factions or are you talking about the public as in humans?"

"Both. The shifters have been quiet, but there're a few humans agitating in town about the wolf pack. Looking for trouble where none exists. It's safer to assume we're always being watched. The priority is to keep the kids safe." Kel shouldered past me but paused before pushing the door open.

"The oven in your cabin is crap. Come down to the lodge kitchen to bake your cookies."

I didn't bother answering—he was already gone. Did this mean I was trapped here at the camp? I wasn't fond of the twenty-first century society but I also wasn't a total hermit. I'd always enjoyed associating with humans even before Armand and his family. The not-aging issue aside, there was very little about me to tip them off that I was not human. I was willing to take precautions but not leaving the camp at all was going to wear on me.

Since I was already in the office, I decided to poke around. What lay behind the door behind the desk and the double doors at the far end of the office?

I chose the double doors first and, as I suspected, they led into a dining hall and kitchen facilities. The kitchen was open to the hall with a half wall separating the two areas. The appliances looked new, the silver chrome kind that attracted handprints. There were two ovens, one the standard type I was familiar with, and the other one of those convection ovens that I stayed well away from. I remembered Agape sneering at me, saying if it hadn't existed in 1943, it still didn't exist for me now. I snarled at the memory. I did not want to talk to her at all, but if she was going to bother Kel, I'd best capitulate and learn to use my phone. I could set the boundaries about how often I had to talk to her.

I opened doors and cupboards, noting the location of things I would need for the cookies. The four fridges contained meat, wild game by the looks of it, and leftover Chinese takeout. There was nothing to drink, and I was glad I had put milk on my list for my baking.

I went back through the office and tried the door behind the front desk. It was open so I slipped in. Better to ask for forgiveness than permission.

I stepped into a large reception room. There was a sizable screen on one wall that I recognized as a modern television. The rest of the walls were adorned with shelves containing books and board games. A corner table had a smaller screen which might be a computer. Still, this was all public fare, maintaining the seasonal camp illusion. Where did the private Kel spend his time? It was terribly nosy, I knew, but I couldn't resist the chance to learn more about him. A hallway led to a small kitchen, a full bathroom, and several bedrooms. Only one showed occupation. Kel's inner sanctum. I stayed at the doorway and looked my fill. I was aware that Kel would be able to tell by scent that I respected his privacy by not going into his bedroom.

The room was tidy, no clothes lying on the floor. An open door on the other side of the room indicated another bathroom. There was nothing to personalize the room: no pictures on the walls or dresser top. Kel could have been using the room for five minutes or five years.

I returned to the lounge and looked for interesting reading material. There were magazines dating back to the fifties. Leafing through them would be a good way to catch up on what I had missed in a more enjoyable way than all those documentaries Agape had tried to make me watch. I sorted them out by decade and had gone through the fifties and sixties when I heard a vehicle pulling up to the office. It was a truck, but it didn't sound like Kel's. I hurried out to the office.

From the owner side of the counter, I could see our visitors through the office window. Four men in camouflage outfits climbed out of a truck that had seen better days. According to their green-brown auras, they were human. I relaxed a bit. Not lykáns, thank goddess, but Kel had told me humans weren't allowed on the property. In lieu of Kel, I was in charge and I would have to do my best to turn them away.

They saw me peering out at them and had a short consultation. Then all four shouldered their way into the office. Three split off in different directions and started fingering the brochures or reading the fake notice board. The fourth who had been the driver stepped up so close to the counter, the edge of it made a dent in his belly.

"Hello, pretty lady." His eyes raked me up and down.

"This is private property. You're trespassing. Please leave or I will have to call the authorities." How, I didn't know. There was no conventional telephone in the office. I needed my cell phone. I could just hear *I told you so* from Kel.

The leader licked his lips. It reminded me of the lizards in the south of France. "No need to be unfriendly, pretty lady. We're looking for permission to do some hunting on your land. Got our licenses and everything. I can show you." He flipped a tag on the counter, but I didn't take my eyes from his.

"This is private property. No hunting allowed." If this got bad, I could flee through the door behind me. I didn't know if it locked, but one of the bathroom doors should.

"You're overrun with wolves, Miss. Your neighbors with cattle and sheep been complaining about what you got going on here. We're offering to thin the pack out a bit. Then they'd be more likely to stay in their own territory. Our licenses let us shoot two each. We'll be in and out before you know it."

I sent out my awareness. There were lykáns in the woods behind the office. I hoped they stayed where they were. I couldn't feel Kel coming back yet. How long did it take to pick up groceries?

"No hunting is allowed on the property. You are not welcome here. Leave. Now." Time to up the pressure. I had made scarier men than this character back down.

The leader of the hunt did not look very intimidated. He sucked his teeth and pivoted on his heel to take in the whole office. "Looks like you don't have much spare change to fix things up nicely. My buds and I would like to make a contribution to the camp. Get yourself a nice couch or one of those expresso machines. Give the place a bit of class."

I crossed my arms. "We don't want your money. I'm calling the police now." I turned and headed for Kel's private quarters. There had to be a phone somewhere. I hoped 9-1-1 worked here in Canada the way it did in Florida.

"Not so fast, Miss Priss." A meaty hand snagged my upper arm. I spun, bent his thumb back, and pushed his hand down until it touched the countertop.

"No touching."

His friends crowded around him. "You want me to take care of her, Matt?" asked one.

"You 'take care' of me, that's assault. I will press charges." I heard a truck pull up in a hurry, gravel slewing. I reached out mentally and touched red fury. Kel was back. "Plus Mr. Hawthorne doesn't like when people harass his staff."

"I don't give a rat's ass…" Matt was interrupted by a large hand grabbing the back of his coat. I let go of his thumb quickly because Matt was travelling. Holding the screen door open with one hand, Kel threw him into the parking lot and then turned to his friends.

"Who's next?"

The one who offered to take care of me swung at Kel's head. Kel caught the flying fist in his own and used the man's momentum to throw him out the door. The remaining two made to run and were helped out of the office with a shove to the back and a boot to the rear.

Kel gave me a dark look and stomped out onto the porch. The hunters were regrouping, picking themselves off the ground and turning to face Kel. I saw one look longingly at the back of the truck, where the guns were, no doubt. Kel just stood there, hands on hips.

"What are you waiting for, Hawthorne? Let's finish this." Matt took off his coat and dropped it on the ground.

"I'm waiting for this," Kel answered and jerked his chin toward the black and white vehicle making its way up to the lodge. It had "O.P.P. Police" written across its hood and on its doors. I ventured out on the porch beside Kel. I could sense the flames of his wrath still simmering. He didn't take his eyes off the men crowding around the policeman as he got out of his cruiser, telling a tale of woe, no doubt. Then I felt his hand touch mine briefly.

"Are you okay? Did any of them hurt you?'

"No. One grabbed my arm, but I took his hand off me."

A low chuckle rumbled through his chest. There was no humor in it. "Yeah, I saw."

The policeman ordered the hunters to go sit in their truck and meandered up to the porch steps. He put one booted foot on the first step as a pose rather than an attempt to join us.

"Kel."

"Dan."

"So, same old, same old?" The policeman flipped a page over in his little notebook and waited with pen poised.

"I'm assuming so. I was in town getting groceries. Found the bunch of them in my office looming over Jo here. She had one in a finger lock on the counter. I removed him from the office and then did the same to his buddies."

The policeman, Dan, turned his eyes to me. "May I have your name, Ma'am?"

I glanced at Kel, and he nodded. "Joanna Kourakis."

"And your position here?"

Should I say empathic dryad healer? No, not today. "Camp counselor."

Policeman Dan wrote that down. "What did the four stooges want from you?"

I didn't understand his reference but answered the general intent of the question. "They wanted permission to hunt wolves on the property. They tried to show me their licenses and said the neighbors with sheep and cattle weren't happy with us."

Kel broke in. "Any complaints that you've heard of, Dan?"

The policeman kept scribbling in his notebook but answered. "None. Wouldn't even know there's a pack up here except for the occasional howling. Most people in town like it. If a cat or small dog goes missing, it's usually a coyote or owl. Never saw any wolf tracks near town."

I relaxed a bit. The lykáns would be crazy to kill livestock or pets around town but they were teenager wolves, and I didn't know how much control Kel had over them. I mentally scanned the forest but the wolves I had sensed there earlier were gone. Policeman Dan interrupted my concentration.

"So, what happened after that, Miz Kourakis?"

"I told them numerous times to leave, that there was no hunting on our private property and threatened to call the police. They didn't take me very seriously. When I tried to go to the safety of Kel's quarters, the one named Matt held my arm so that I couldn't leave. The one with the bad beard asked if Matt wanted him to take care of me."

The policeman muttered something under his breath

then looked at Kel. "So, charges of trespassing. You want assault added to that?"

"Trespassing should be good enough. There's no camera in the office to confirm the assault, and it will end up a big argument in court. Oh, and damage to property. They jammed the gate open. Must have been hiding in the bush, waiting for me to leave and then ran out to stick a pry bar in the hinge. That's a couple of thousand right there to fix."

Policeman Dan snapped his notebook shut. "I'll charge these yahoos and escort them off the property. You know they have hunting blinds set up all along the border of the Carsen property and yours? If the wolves step off your land, they're fair game."

Kel scratched his beard stubble. "Nothing I can do about that, but I think the wolves will smell the pot reek and stay away."

"Yeah. There's that. Have a nice day, you two."

"Thanks," I mumbled. It was alarming to hear that the humans were just waiting to blast a wolf that stepped out of line. If it were spring, I could make a line of vines and thorns grow around their hiding places. No matter how much they chopped, they would always come back. But it was winter, and everything was sleeping.

"Come help me unload," Kel ordered, and I obediently trotted behind him to the truck. He handed me a couple of plastic bags. Then he took the rest up, at least ten bags per hand. A casual display of lykán strength. I'm sure it was for the benefit of the hunters who were still talking to the policeman from their truck.

"I thought you'd never get back," I told him as I held the office door open for him.

"I was longer because I couldn't find your damn

blanched almonds at the first store. I had to go to the next town with the bigger store."

I jumped ahead of him to open the double doors to the hall and kitchen. We made swift work of putting the groceries away. I only had to ask him twice where things went, and he pointed rather than speaking. It began to dawn on me that Kel was angry at me. Once the last box was away, except for the things I was taking to my cabin, I dared to put a hand on his arm.

"I'm sorry if you're mad at me but I can't think of anything else I could have done."

He spun on me and backed me up against a counter. He held up his hand with the back of it facing me. He started ticking off things on his fingers.

"One, run. Two, run. Three…"

I pulled his hand down. "I get the idea, but I was still in the office, and I wouldn't have been able to get past them without immediate violence. I was trying to talk my way out of the situation."

"Why were you still in the office?"

I sighed. "I was snooping around after you left. Checking out this hall and the private lounge. Plus, your quarters." I waited for a blast as to why I had invaded his privacy, but it didn't come. I realized I was still holding his hand and let go of it quickly. "I will confess to regretting my stance about portable phones. Had I had mine on me and known how to use it, I would have called you and the police. I'll remedy that tonight."

Kel backed away from me and picked up the bags containing my groceries. "Okay."

"Okay? That's it?"

"Sure. You were honest about why you were still in the office when they came. You admitted a cell phone would have helped, and you're going to fix that. You didn't know they were trouble and now you do. So next time…?"

"Run."

"Yes, or…?

I thought about it for a moment. "Oh. Vanish into the walls."

"Bingo. Let's get these up to your cabin."

I was glad to see both hunters' truck and police vehicle gone from the parking lot, so we didn't have to walk by them again. "Why are they so insistent on shooting wolves? If I hadn't been here, would they have tried to shoot a wolf before you got back?"

"No, I think they were just getting the lay of the land. No time for a hunt before I got back. They're cautious of me as I've already told them to keep off the property. They didn't expect you. Technically this is a summer camp for at risk kids. Only the caretaker should be around and that's me."

I opened my cabin door for him. "What would they gain by intimidating me?"

"Maybe get you to say yes. Then they would have come later, probably through the property from the Carsen land. Try and bag some wolves fast and get out. Then claim you told them they could."

"What happens when a lykán is killed in wolf form?"

Kel was making quick work of stowing my groceries. "Stays a wolf. Our secret would be protected." He put my milk in the refrigerator and jammed the plastic shopping bags into his pocket. "I have to see about getting someone in to fix the gate. Don't forget to bring your cookies down to the lodge to cook them. I don't trust this oven."

"Okay. Thanks for helping me, Kel."

He snorted. "Although I would prefer you had run, you were doing fine on your own. These guys must be nothing after the Gestapo. See you at dinner."

He left, closing the door gently behind him. I stood frozen in place. He knew about my past. Min must have been talking. I felt a wave of disappointment pass through me. I thought I could start anew here but it would be all "poor Jo" and her tragic past. I kicked a little plastic garbage can and sent it rolling. I also said a few bad words in French.

****

At precisely five o'clock I lugged all my cookie-making materials down to the lodge. Kel wasn't in the office, so I went right on through to the dining hall. There were five teens in human form in hoodies and sweatpants playing a card game at one of the dining tables. Evan was one of them. I nodded a greeting as I made my way to the kitchen. There was a large pot on top of the stove that smelled delicious. The sauce for the spaghetti, no doubt.

I preheated the oven and prepared my little section of counter. I combined the almonds, sugar, egg whites, and vanilla extract in a food processor. That was one invention that I wished I'd had in 1943. I pulsed it to do the initial mixing and then ran it for two minutes. All the teens stopped playing their game and stared at me until I had finished. Too bad, *mes petites*, interruptions must be tolerated for the sake of cookies. I had forgotten to ask Kel to get me a pastry bag with a wide tip nozzle, so I cut a hole in the corner of a freezer bag and squeezed the batter out into one-inch mounds. The freezer bag technique lacked finesse, and I could hear Madame

Chenier's chiding. I mentally promised her I would do a big stock up of proper baking equipment if I could persuade Kel to break his nobody-leaves rule and take me shopping.

The batter had to sit fifteen minutes. The kids were ignoring me, so I went back to the office and through to the private lounge. I grabbed some of the magazines I had been reading and brought them back to the kitchen.

The cookies were ready for the oven, and I popped them in. I leaned against the counter and leafed through the magazine. The almond smell of the cookies filled the room, and I saw the teens' noses twitching. My timer went off, and I pulled the cooked macarons out. Perfect. Crisp on the outside and they would be chewy on the inside. As I transferred them to racks to cool, Kel sauntered into the dining hall. He came to a dramatic halt and sniffed the air heavily.

"What's that smell?"

"Are you being rude? It's my cookies."

He was in the kitchen, crowding me, trying to reach around me for a cookie. I slapped his hand.

"After dinner or you'll ruin your appetite. Also, I have to dust them with confectioner's sugar." My mouth fell open in a gasp as he picked me up and set me down several feet away. He was back at the cookies before I could gather further protest, shoving one into his mouth.

"And?" I asked. "Good enough for apex predators?"

"Hell, yes. But you didn't make enough." Crumbs showered down the front of his flannel shirt as he spoke.

I frowned at the racks. "I made three dozen. How many kids are you expecting?"

Kel nodded at the teens playing cards. "These stay in skin for dinner and card games. We might see the eight who will change only to eat. Don't expect them to talk to you. There may be some who come in fur, but don't let them eat any human food. They have to change first."

I wondered how I was going to stop a wolf if he or she wanted a cookie. "And three dozen aren't enough cookies for thirteen kids and two adults?"

"It's enough for me. If you won't make more, the kids can fend for themselves."

"Hey!" Evan said. "Sharing is caring, Uncle Kel."

I sighed. "I'll make some more after dinner. It's almost six, and you have to make the main meal."

Kel nudged me out of the kitchen. "Go play cards. I just have to put a pot of hot water on for the spaghetti and dump pre-cooked meatballs into the sauce. Ten minutes."

I walked with more confidence than I felt over to the kids. "Deal me in?"

There was a cringeful pause, then Evan moved aside on the bench so I could sit down. "Do you know how to play euchre, Anna-Jo?"

"I think I know. Refresh me on the rules."

****

It had been a good dinner. I made more cookies until I ran out of ingredients. Four who would change but not talk came, and I made sure a plate was in reach. A beautiful red wolf begged me for a cookie, and I almost broke down. But then Kel interjected firmly.

"Only if you change, Beth. People food is for those in skin."

I was disappointed that she would rather do without the cookie than change but there would be other spaghetti nights. I decided to try and remember the other Christmas cookie recipes from the bakery. The kids said they would help me search on the internet for the ones I couldn't recall. They charged my phone and made me look at my messages. They walked me through calling Agape, and we all rolled our eyes together as she yelled at me. I saw Kel bristling out of the corner of my eye and put a halt to her tirade. We bartered one call, once a week, and I hung up well-pleased with myself. Then the kids loaded a strange game on my phone with irate birds and supercilious pigs.

The kids were still playing cards when I decided to call it a night. Kel walked me up to my cabin, and I decided to call him on his comment about the Gestapo.

"So, how much do you know about my past?"

"Min told me what happened." He had a habit of scrubbing his stubble when he didn't want to participate in a conversation. I persisted.

"Everything?"

"I'm not sure what 'everything' entails. I'm sorry you lost your boyfriend. And I'm sorry you've had a hard time of it since you've woken up."

There was more sympathy than pity in his tone. "Thank you."

"No problem. I've changed my mind about letting you go to town. You've already been seen by the biggest mouths around here. We can get you used to modern civilization by way of small Northern Ontario towns. And you did good with the kids tonight."

I fanned myself with my hand. "All these compliments. Have you had too much sugar, Kel?"

"Must be it. Here you are, safely home. Pleasant dreams."

I smiled without answering. I could hope to skip my nightmares but after the confrontation with the hunters, I would probably be trapped in them all night. I gave him a little salute and went into my cabin. The day had ended well. I could hold on to that.

****

I was having the dream again, but it was different this time. I was creeping along the embankment with my explosives but now it was wolves who were with me, not humans. I stopped and tried to shoo them off, but we were already at the hole. Gunfire erupted all around us, and the wolves went down. A bullet hit the explosives I was carrying, and then all was fire.

I woke up to a wet rasping on my face. I raised my hand to stop the annoyance, and the sensation transferred to my hand. I blinked my eyes to clear them. There was a huge gray wolf in bed with me.

"Kel! You were not invited."

Kel did not seem perturbed. Instead, he turned his back to me and snuggled backwards until the whole length of him lay against me. He was too big to shove out of bed, and I did not want to sleep on the couch when I had a comfortable bed. And I was just too tired. I pulled my pillow down under my head and fell asleep.

****

When I woke up, the sun was long risen. I had learned to use my phone as a clock and saw it was eight thirty, a whole hour later than I usually awoke. Someone was banging around in my kitchen, and I could smell bacon. I threw on some clothes and went to talk to my intruder.

Kel was at my stove, dressed in his usual uniform of flannel shirt and jeans. He glanced over his shoulder as I approached.

"Eggs and bacon suit you? It'll be ready in a few

minutes."

I sat down at the little two-seater table which I hadn't used yet. I stared at Kel's back, trying to bore two holes with my eyes alone, but he was oblivious. A large helping of the aforementioned eggs and bacon was plunked down in front of me.

"I can't eat all this," I told him.

He sat opposite me with an even larger helping. "What you can't eat, Evan and the others will be happy to take care of for you."

I ate a mouthful. It was delicious. "So," I said once I had swallowed. "Do you make a habit of rescuing small woodland creatures?"

"Sure. The ones that I don't intend on eating."

"I don't need to be babysat. That's what drove me crazy in the Grove."

"It's not babysitting. You have bad dreams. A lot of the kids have that so they sleep in a pile of wolves who can wake them up and comfort them if that happens. I'm just doing the same for you." His plate was almost clean. The man ate like a machine.

"Kel."

"Jo."

"How did you get in? I'm sure I locked the door."

He pulled a key from his jean's pocket. "Master key."

"Ah." Of course. "I guess there's no way to stop you then, even if you weren't invited."

"No. But in your bed, I stay in fur." He raised intense amber eyes to mine. "Skin when I'm invited."

Oh. Right. I hadn't been sure how to interpret those glances but now I knew.

"Not sure I'm ready for that yet." My body was, but

my mind still remembered Armand.

"Take your time. I'm in no rush. Can you eat anymore?" I shook my head, and he picked up both our plates. Scraping the rest of the skillet's contents onto my plate, he went to the front door and set it on the porch. "Come and get it!" There was a flurry of clicking toenails.

After twenty seconds, Kel picked up a spotless plate and brought it to the sink to wash along with the other dishes. I was being lazy.

"Hey, let me finish that. You must have things you need to get done today."

"Just the gate." He cleaned the skillet and stacked it in a rack to dry. "You want to go for a walk, go ahead. The kids will keep you company."

"Now it's okay to go for a walk in the woods?"

He made a show of looking out the kitchen window. "You might have figured out by now that I like keep things under control. I've now decided that you can be safe charging all over the woods, provided the kids are with you."

Kel certainly had trouble admitting he was wrong. "That's very kind of you," I said straight-faced. I liked the idea of Kel looking out for me as long as he didn't hold too tightly. I must have drifted off thinking about being held tightly because Kel called my name.

I snapped out it. "Sorry, what did you say?"

"I asked if you were okay."

"Yeah." I smiled at him. "Got a lot to think about." Like how a strange combination of dryad and lykán could possibly work.

His reciprocating smile took my breath away. "You do that. See you later."

I sat at that little table for quite a while.

****

The countdown to Christmas went quickly. Every Monday night I made the almond macarons plus another traditional French cookie. There were more kids each time, and Beth even changed for a few minutes to eat her human food cookie. Each night there was a wolf in my bed. A few nights each week Kel was busy, but he sent Evan and Amy in his stead. They ignored my protests that I was perfectly fine and curled up at the foot of my bed, noses under tails. They did not, however, make me breakfast. And I stopped having bad dreams.

I asked Kel what the camp normally did for Christmas. As preternatural creatures, we, or our lineages predated Christ, but when in Rome… Kel rubbed his stubble and, for the first time since I had known him, looked embarrassed.

"I cook a couple of turkeys, with stuffing, do some veggies. Buy pies from the supermarket. I throw up some lights. I didn't think you'd like a real tree so I'm buying a fake one tomorrow."

Oh my. Santa Kel. "I'll take care of the pies for you. And yes, you're right about not having the amputated corpse of a tree in the lodge. What about presents?"

'Erm," said Kel, clearing his throat. "Don't really deal with that."

"You could get clothes for the ones who wear skin and hit the pet stores for chewies for all. I can make a list for you."

"No, you're coming with me. I'm not enduring this agony alone."

"Okay," I said, trying to hide a triumphant grin.

"I know I was manipulated into that."

I was eager to go make my lists and danced to the lodge's door. "Hey, I'm just a timid forest creature. No way could I make an alpha like you do anything you didn't want to."

"Nothing is without a price," he said ominously.

"I'll gladly pay it," I shouted over my shoulder.

****

Shopping was amazing. We went to the next closest town because it had a big box store, and I went crazy with Kel's credit card. I was shocked at the prices of things, but Kel told me they were less than other stores. A woman accosted us, but it turned out she was on the town council and wanted something from Kel as a local businessman. I let my attention wander and thought I caught sight of someone familiar, but then my focus was jerked back to the woman who was reaching for the disc around my neck.

"Oh, how lovely. Where did you get it?" She laid a fingertip on it, and I shuddered at the shocking intimacy. I made some sort of squeak, and then Kel was pulling me to his side in a naturally affectionate gesture.

"Family heirloom," he told her, showing a bit too much tooth. The woman quickly excused herself, frightened but not knowing why.

Eager to dismiss the incident, I turned to leave the aisle, and my eyes met those of Matt Holloway. He had a smirk on his face, and I wondered what he had seen that pleased him so much.

"Kel, possible trouble," I murmured.

Again, he stood close to me, putting his body between me and Holloway. The hunter gave a snippy little wave and disappeared into the hunting and fishing section.

We finished our shopping, each of us pushing a full cart, and I didn't see Holloway again. We were bound to run into him in the small communities, but I was glad I had been with Kel. I wasn't going to ask to go into town by myself anytime soon. Not that Kel would let me.

We headed back to the lodge, through the newly fixed gate, and unloaded the most food I had ever seen in one place. We hid the presents in one of the lodge's spare bedrooms after Kel assured me that the kids didn't use them. They preferred to sleep in one of the cabins, if they weren't in the pack dens. Or at the foot of my bed.

I was in a good mood when I retired to my cabin. It had been spaghetti and meatballs night and Kel and I had put up the fake tree, decorated it and hung some Christmas lights on the wall of the dining hall. The kids had rolled their eyes at it all but tolerated it. I noticed that two more of the change-only-to-eat-people-food group stayed in skin to play some cards. Beth got her macaron and a madeleine for changing, but I knew it would be a long road before she was one of the card-playing teens.

I made some proper hot chocolate, stirring milk over the stove. It suddenly struck me that I hadn't thought about Armand for a while. Or, if I thought of him in the context of the bakery, those memories didn't bring me pain. I didn't dwell on his death anymore, either. Goddess bless Aunt Min. She knew this would be good for me.

There was a scratching at the door, and I let Kel in. He sniffed regretfully at the hot chocolate aroma. He had come in fur and wasn't going to change into skin. Unless…

"You get into bed. I'll bring you a mug of hot chocolate."

Kel snorted. He didn't break his own rule about eating people food in fur.

I knelt and took his heavy snout in my hands. "You're invited."

He froze, his amber eyes staring into mine.

"Yes, I mean it. Get going."

He vanished into the bedroom with a flick of his tail, even as it was morphing into a bare, furless butt.

He never got to drink his hot chocolate.

****

It was strange waking up with a person rather than a wolf. I felt a moment of panic. I had changed the rules, the dynamics of our relationship. What if it didn't work out? He'd make me go, and I didn't want to leave. This was home.

"Stop thinking so hard, Jo. There's smoke coming out of your ears."

"No there isn't." I rolled toward him. His eyes were intent on my face, and I saw worry there. I couldn't bear his uncertainty, so I kissed it out of him. That led to other things that could have gone on all morning but for a sharp bark outside our window.

"That's Evan. He's reminding us that it's Christmas Eve and there's work to be done."

"When did Evan the slacker become Evan the taskmaster?" I groaned and stretched luxuriously. I whined like a complaining puppy when Kel slid out of bed, taking his warmth with him.

He smiled down at me. "You've almost got that right. Just a little yip at the end."

"Stay," I coaxed.

"I can see why all those ancient Greeks and their gods liked the dryads so much. I didn't know what I was missing."

"Not even with Min?" I had wondered about that. Min had quite the libido.

"Never went there. Never wanted to. She went to town if she had the itch." He bent down and kissed me to stop my protest. "Yeah, I know. Different rules for her, but who could stop Minerva from doing what she wanted?"

"Nobody," I agreed.

"Not jealous then?"

"No. Unless there's a hidden lykán mate you haven't been telling me about, Mr. Rochester."

"Nope, Miss Eyre. I really got to get going. You'll be okay?"

I stretched again. "Fine and dandy. I'll be down to start the pies to get a leg up on things. See you then."

Kel shimmered and shifted into a wolf. I remembered he had come that way and would not have any clothes to wear. He could work the door latch with his teeth, so I stayed in bed a bit longer. I felt good. The nagging feeling that I had rushed into something was gone. I released a long breath. I was finally leaving the past behind.

****

Because it was Christmas Eve, the kids gathered in the lodge as if it were a Monday night. If Kel and I wanted to hide our new relationship status, we were doomed from the start. Maybe it was the way we studiously avoided looking at each other or touching. Or, most likely, they could smell us on each other. I saw Amy whispering in Evan's ear, and he nodded.

"Kel-meister and Anna-Jo, you are excused early tonight. I'll see to turning out the lights and locking up."

"Really, Evan that's not necessary" My protest was interrupted by Kel grabbing my hand and handing me my coat.

We were halfway out the door when Kel paused us for a moment. "Thanks, Evan. We'll see you guys tomorrow for Christmas dinner. Don't eat any wild game. There'll be plenty of food, so I want you hungry. And hands off the pies. They're for tomorrow."

"Night," I called but Kel had already pulled me out the door.

"Kel."

"Jo."

"This is a bit unseemly." It seemed I wasn't going fast enough for him because he picked me up and strode up the road to my cabin.

"Unseemly is my middle name."

****

I lay on Kel's warm chest and watched the fire burn down. We hadn't made it to the bedroom this time, but Kel had made a nest of pillows and blankets in front of the fire that did perfectly fine for us.

"You okay?" Kel's question woke me out of a doze.

"Sure." After our love making, how could I be anything else?

"No, I mean are you okay here."

I leaned up on one elbow to look at his face. "Here as in Camp Dyre?"

"Yeah."

I smiled. "I love it here."

He didn't smile back. "There's a lot going on here that you haven't seen yet. Clan politics, what to do with the kids who reach their majority and can't integrate back into Clan society, how to fend off my own clan who think I am wasting my time here. A whole lot going on."

I stroked his cheek. "I want to help. The kids are great, and they deserve everything that we can do for them."

"What about me?" He asked, rolling on top of me. "Do you think I'm great, too?"

"Well…" He silenced me with a kiss. I ran my fingers up through his hair and returned the kiss enthusiastically. Then a shot rang out. Very close.

"Kel!"

He was up and then pulling me up as well. "Stay in the cabin. Lock the door. Please. I'll handle this. If necessary, hide in the walls. We've planned for something like this. We'll be all right."

"But…"

"Please. I can't concentrate if you're not safe." At my reluctant nod, he shimmered into the wolf.

I put one hand on his shoulder. "Wait a second. Let me see who's out there." I sent my mind out into the dark and touched greed and vile excitement. "Holloway and his three friends. Be careful. They don't care what damage they do. They're too worked up."

Kel licked my hand, and I opened the door for him. He was gone in a flash, and I obediently locked the door behind him. More shots rang out, and I yelped. They were shooting at the kids or Kel. I could kill them if I had to, but then we'd have to explain how Matt Holloway got halfway inside a tree. I ran to the bedroom and put on some warm clothes. I still might have to go outside, and I wanted to be ready.

I was pulling on my boots when the window in the living room smashed. I screamed as a bottle with flame coming out of the neck was flung into the room. It smashed on the floor and blue flames licked out across the wood planks. The wood caught fire, and the cabin filled with black smoke. I cursed. My phone was in the bedroom, but I might not survive retrieving it. *Sorry, Kel, but it's leave or get cooked*, I thought and ran out the front door.

It was chaos outside. Two other cabins were on fire, but the lodge seemed intact. The flickering shapes of wolves darting through the trees were caught in the uncertain light of the fire that was consuming my cabin.

The best thing for me to do would be to get over to a big old white pine. I could hide inside and keep my promise to Kel to stay safe. I ran from tree to tree, trying to not to be out in the open for too long. If the hunters shot an apparent human, they'd be in prison for a long time but that would be no consolation to me. I could see the pine of choice and sent out a quick mental search to locate the hunters.

Two were over by cabin two. One was out in the woods. He was finally becoming worried. Things weren't going as planned. Wolves weren't supposed to fight back like this. The fourth…was behind me.

"Gotcha," Holloway said as his beefy forearm went across my neck. "Wouldn't want you to get in the way of our wolf hunt. You know where Hawthorne is?"

I couldn't answer, he was choking me. He must have realized it because the pressure on my throat eased.

"Get out now," I told him "and they might let you live." Hopefully, that would start putting doubt in his mind, cut through the blood lust.

"It'll be them who die." He switched his chokehold to a brutal grip on my hair. "I got some plastic ties in the truck. Gonna put you where you can't cause trouble."

I hardened my nails to bark and reached up, slashing at the wrist of the hand that held my hair. Holloway cursed but, to my dismay, did not let go of me. A punch to the face brought me to my knees and left me stunned. I felt his hand fumbling at my neck. I screamed as I felt my disc and its leather thong lift from around my neck.

"Yeah, thought this meant something to you. How about you cooperate, or I'll throw this on the fire right now."

I couldn't become a hostage to this man. It would cripple Kel's fight against the hunters. I thought about the cyanide capsules we carried as Resistance fighters. Well, there were different ways of committing suicide.

"Stick it up your ass for all I care," I snarled and lunged upwards to claw at his eyes. He jerked his head back, and I missed my target. His backhand was more panicked this time, but it did its job. I stumbled backward and went flying over a pile of stacked wood.

"Have it your way, bitch," he told me and threw my disc on the flaming ruin of my cabin. I shrieked in agony. The Gestapo had taken my disc when I was captured but they hadn't destroyed it. The French dryads had recovered it when they rescued me. Its temporary absence had weakened me and slowed my healing, but this was a thousand times worse.

Something big flew out of the woods and hit Holloway with a solid thump. He went down without a sound. I saw the wolf shaking him by the throat and heard the crack of his neck breaking. I tried to get up, but my legs wouldn't support me. My vision was failing as well, but my mind touched Kel's. Of course, he'd come to my rescue.

I must have blacked out for a moment. There was

warm wolf breath on my face, and I looked into Kel's amber eyes. "He burnt my disc," I whispered. "I don't know why but I'm fading fast. I should have had plenty of time to get back to my tree."

I didn't hear his answer because everything went dark again. After that, I woke up a few times. The first, I was being carried, my cheek against a bare chest, and then laid in the back seat of Kel's truck, my head in someone's lap. I touched Evan's mind and then Kel's.

"What are you doing," I mumbled.

Evan bent over me. "Taking you to your tree, Anna-Jo."

"Too far," I told him. It was. Three days to Florida was too long. I would be gone before then.

"We'll get there. We called Agape for help. She said once we get below the snow line, the trees will be awake, and we can get an old one to lend you some energy. Now go to sleep and save your strength."

"Was anyone hurt?" I asked.

"We lost Beth and Kyle." I gave a whimper when I heard that. "Kel killed Holloway but made it look like a fall and a broken neck. The rest of Holloway's buddies ran off, but we know who they are. If they don't get charged with arson and trespassing, we'll sue them into the ground. One way or another, there will be hell to pay for Beth and Kyle."

"Hell to pay." I echoed.

"Go to sleep, Anna-Jo. You're out of it."

So, I did.

****

I woke when someone splashed cold water in my face. I blearily opened my eyes and saw Kel and Evan squatting in front of me. My back was against rough bark.

Kel touched my face to get my attention. "Jo, there's an old oak behind you. You need to take some strength from it."

"Too tired," I told him. I was. It was time to let things go.

Kel gave me a sharp shake, making my head bob. My eyes flew open.

"Jo, do what you're told for once. I'm not losing you."

"Let me go, Kel." I was so tired.

"Nope." He kissed me. I hummed against his lips. I was so lucky to have known him.

"Yuck. You guys." Evan interrupted us. "Please Anna-Jo. I want you to live. Taste that big old oak."

"Okay." I couldn't bear the pain in his voice. I reached out and found the oak's mellow strength flowing all around me. It was trying to help and was waiting for me to notice. I carefully drew some power into me and immediately felt better. "Oh, that's nice."

"Take some more," Kel urged.

"Not too much more or I'll hurt the tree." A few more sips, and I could hold up my head on my own. "Where are we?"

"North Carolina." Kel reached behind and brought out a brown bag with a logo on it. "Can you eat something?"

I thought about it and my stomach roiled. "No."

"Do you have to relieve yourself? No? Then, let's get going." He handed the bag to Evan who started rooting around in it. Gathering me in his arms, he lifted me effortlessly and deposited me in the back of the truck. The floor was covered with wrappers and cups.

I wanted to comment on their housekeeping, but my eyes were easing shut again. I heard Kel call to Evan to hurry up, and then I was gone.

****

"Jo, wake up."

I groaned and squeezed my eyes shut. I felt bad again, not quite as bad as before the oak tree. Someone took my hand and pressed it against the smooth trunk of a tree. Oh! My tree.

"We're here?"

"Yeah, open your eyes."

I obeyed but it took a few moments to focus. I was in Kel's arms. His stubble had grown alarmingly into a beard. Evan stood just beyond him, his eyes red and sunken. None of us smelled that great. There were people around us, and I blearily recognized Agape and the other Grove sisters.

"Joanna, you need to get into your tree." Agape was bossy as ever.

"No, just stay here. Touching. Don't need to go in."

"Yes, you do, Grove sister. Your disc being burned affected you more severely than it should have. You obviously weren't fully recovered. I blame myself for not realizing this and sending you out into danger that you were not able to handle." Agape was on a roll.

"Oh, for the sake of the goddess." I buried my face in Kel's neck to hide from her. Maybe if I couldn't see her, she didn't exist.

Kel turned his head to speak to Agape. "I appreciate all your assistance in getting Jo back home alive but you're not helping right now. So back off, lady."

I gave a little laugh that was more of a wheeze when I heard Agape's gasp of insult.

"Now, sweetheart, you're going in." He shifted me higher in his grip and pushed me closer to my tree. "You need to get better."

"No," I protested.

"Why not?"

I was silent but a familiar voice spoke up. "The last time she went in a tree, she was there for seventy years, and the world she knew was gone." Aunt Min was there.

Agape harrumphed. "She won't need to be in that long. Weeks only. Maybe months."

"I don't care. I'm not going in. I'm not losing everything." They couldn't force me in. Only I could make my tree open for me.

"Jo." Kel stroked my cheek, and I looked at him. "I'll be here when you get out."

"No, you can't do that. You have responsibilities at the camp. The kids need you."

He kissed my cheekbone. "The clans have stepped up, especially ones who have a kid at Dyre. There're several volunteers looking after the place until I can get back. The Conclave lawyers are handling the issue of the Holloway and his buddies. Now get in that tree."

Aunt Min leaned over his shoulder. "Trust him, darling girl. He won't let you down."

I wanted to live so I had to believe Kel would be there when I emerged. "Okay." I sighed.

Kel propped me against my tree, and I slid into its depths, feeling the joyful pulse of recognition from my beautiful poplar. I fought another stab of fear that made me want to fling myself back into Kel's arms and let myself sink in the depths of sleep.

****

It was like a birth. I slid from the warmth of my tree,

but instead of flopping onto the ground at the base of my tree, I was caught up in strong arms and a soft robe was wrapped around me. Something was slipped over my head to rest on my throat. I reached up and touched a wooden disc.

"Kel?" I felt so much better but still wobbly.

"Right here, Jo."

"How long?" Had he been waiting by my tree all this time?

"Three weeks and a few days. And no, I wasn't sleeping under your tree the whole time." Had I said that out loud? "Your sisters gave me some space in the Grove Hall. They said they could tell when you were ready to come out. Can you stand?" He let my feet touch the ground, and I was able to hold myself upright.

"You waited for me." I couldn't get over that.

"Of course, I did. I'll always be here for you."

I kissed him with all my heart.

"Guys? Yuck. Get a room."

Kel broke off the kiss but put his lips to my temple. "I asked for privacy, Evan."

"And we gave it to you. But now there are phone calls to make to our pack, road trips to plan, and cookies to bake."

"Mmm, cookies," I whispered in his ear. "That's how I got you to fall in love with me."

He gave me a quelling glance. "I fell in love with you the day you got out of that ridiculously expensive SUV, driven by that ridiculously horny satyr, told me you didn't want the Wi-Fi password and threatened to keep us all in line with a rolled-up newspaper."

"That would do it, too."

"But the cookies didn't hurt."

I wrapped my arms around him and kissed him soundly, Evan's gagging noises only a dim noise in the background, like the buzzing of a fly.